Something's Not Right

a collection of speculative fiction short stories.

yves.

interior text is set in sylfaen. cover text is set in arial, rudiment (by kevin richey), and roddy (by john romero iv). cover image by annie spratt on unsplash.

happy birthday, avi kaplan-lipkin.

(january 8th, 2000)

1. Romance—Fiction. 2. Children—Fiction. 3. Monsters—Fiction?

isbn-10: 1978485867

isbn-13: 978-1978485860

a dedication.

to a Reader who has been steadfast, brave, true, and indomitable in the face of my most controversial opinions. he is kind, and funny, and has dark curly hair that is always parted a little bit west of uniform, and because he is not very good on picking up on the finer points of implied text i will let him know that i am, in fact, referring to him, avi kaplan-lipkin, who is responsible for most of the work shown here.

SOMETHING'S NOT RIGHT

contents.

sorted somewhat by length, in a roundabout way. occasionally things fall into chronological order, though I must assure you that it occurs each time by accident. of course, you don't have to believe me.

preface.

the title of this book was taken from a much longer phrase, which i have loved since i first heard it: "the nagging feeling that something's not right."

this book is based around the genre of speculative fiction, which is rather difficult to explain. it is, in its most distilled essence, realistically-written fiction which contains fantasy or science fiction elements without actually becoming either of those genres, but of course this explanation is not quite as palatable as others might be. here i offer one alternative:

speculative fiction is about almost all things being normal, but some things being not quite so. you wouldn't normally encounter different breeds of vampires in your daily life, but if you did, and if they were just a normal part of your day, speculative fiction would capture them perfectly. in speculative fiction, everything is sort of taken in stride; things are as they are now, with some minor adjustments.

the stories in this collection are rather widely inclusive of the different kinds of speculative fiction. there are some that are fantasy-leaning speculative fiction, there are some that are science fiction-leaning speculative fiction. there are some that are essentially science fiction or fantasy with a little yves. stamp on them, and there are some that don't fit into any label directly. there is not one singular world (in most cases) that unites them. they range in size from one page to almost twenty. this makes categorizing them with a singular concept rather difficult.

that being said: my hope is, by the end of this book, these scenarios will stop sending you the nagging feeling that something's not right. i am hoping that someone, somewhere, may read this and discover a deep-seated love for all things considered improper, and with that in mind, i gave this collection its name.

most monstrous regards,

yves.

base.

"You must be lost," she says.

He comes forward a little farther out of the shade, blinking in the sudden sun, and leans one arm against a tree trunk. There's a leaf tucked into the collar of his shirt (which leans, one size too large, halfway across one shoulder), and there's dirt on his jeans.

"What makes you say that?" he asks, rubbing his cheek. He's on the pale side, and his tousled hair looks like rust on wood; he has a smear of something green on one cheek. His eyes are tired.

"Well," she says, "One. You're dressed out of fashion."

He looks down at his clothes (dark brown cross between a sweater and a real shirt; jeans that are too baggy and not baggy enough; shoes? not really) and back up at her. He smiles.

"Two. You're in the wrong place, for this time of day."

He watches her, and she walks towards him, stepping around the thorns. There is long grass, and she flattens it; sparse flowers, and she crushes them.

"Three," she says, and she takes his face in her hands. He puts his hands to hers, and he's too soft; he looks inviting. "I'm hungry, and I *only* eat lost things."

1

gifted child.

Aspen frowned and looked up into the sky. It was going to rain.

Their father-parent looked at them oddly. They looked up at him and shrugged one shoulder, hair fluttering slightly in the wind.

"Going to rain," they said, and he nodded.

"Clairvoyancy?" he asked. They bent down and picked up a penny from the ground—heads.

"Just the clouds."

He sat down beside them, tracing a small circle around himself in the dust. Aspen glanced at him, and he looked at them. They sighed and flicked the penny at him.

"Good job," he said, catching it so heads faced him. "Again."

They tossed it up in the air, and he caught it, covering it with his hands.

"Which one?" he asked, and they cocked their head.

"Tails," they said, and concentrated. He paused, looking up at the sky. There was a shiver from the coin in his hand. "Now heads."

Aspen's parent-father opened his hands and revealed the coin—on heads.

"Good job," he murmured. Aspen closed their hand, and he watched as the penny slowly disappeared from his. He could already guess where it had gone, and when Aspen opened their fist, he was only surprised to find two pennies rather than one. Aspen smirked, and he waved his hand at them, vaguely trying to articulate the problem. "You—haven't learned creation yet. Or duplication."

"I had it in my pocket," Aspen said, and closed their hand again. "Let's go inside."

Their father-parent opened his mouth to ask why, but stopped when he felt the rain.

the turning of claribella holte.

And she was sitting inside, and it was dark. The white gauze blew against the window. Strands of hair, illuminated gently by the outside light, half-heartedly freed themselves from her braid. Her necklace glittered. In the shadows, her white dress became soft and transparent, and the top two buttons lay unbuttoned, exposing a section of dull-rose skin.

And she had arched eyebrows, brown and thin, which made her look more bemused than serious. Her ear curled in to the soft shape of her jaw, and the wet lines of shadow on her skin followed through to her down-turned lips. One hand, beringed, rested in her lap, and the other waited patiently along her side. Her legs were curled and bent beneath her, and their sharp reflections were elegant in the dark.

And outside, there were white roses, planted in deep-dark soil. There was a soft breeze up, slowly detaching petals, and a rough bootprint that lodged the petals in the earth.

And all of these things were true, and simultaneous, and all of them were occurring only a moment before she might be killed, and rise again.

4

unconditional.

The thunder arrives, knocking against the windows and walls, and I know he will be here soon. He only comes in the storms, when it is black enough, wet enough, loud enough to obscure the world. My father caught a glimpse of him once, through the pane of glass, and now he starts when he hears a noise in the rain, walking without purpose to the shotgun that hangs on his bedroom wall. But my father cannot catch him. The gun is not made for heavenly things.

When I put my hand, long ago, to his halo *(it is so wide, a hollow moon of light and caught breath)* it came back bleeding; I had cut myself. He apologized, running one hand over the wound *(i think he has so many hands, there are too many to count, but when i look i only see two),* and within the minute it was gone and the air near my skin sparkled with an excitement almost matching mine.

Now I find a drop of blood on my bedspread.

"good evening"

His weight shifts the bed and it lists to one side, so he positions himself to sit on the blanket just beside me, closer to the middle. When I am near him, I am full of mirrors; light comes from my eyes and mouth, and I cannot speak. I touch the blindfold he wears tonight instead, questioning. He does not answer, but pulls away, and I know: he is hiding his face, and his lack of eyes. It is strange to have someone like him so afraid of me. With one hand, I tell him that he shouldn't be; I reach up behind his face and untie the cloth.

my parents are spies.

I didn't realize at first, but now that I have, it's impossible to forget.

There's a way that they look at me: first out of the corner of their eyes, measuring, then with a false concern when I catch their gaze. As if they're worried about me, because why would I need to look at them? Is everything okay?

I was the first in my family to grow wings—that I know of, I guess. They were painful, and itched where the feathers were coming in, and I started wearing baggier shirts and using duct tape to strap the hollow bones against my body. When I looked online, I found advice—things like professional wing-hiders, wing paint that promised to hide them from view. *NEVER USE DUCT TAPE,* one site read, in angry, caps-lock warning. *YOUR WINGS MAY BREAK AND YOUR SPINE MAY SUFFER PERMANENT DAMAGE.*

There's anger in the news. Things about this new trend, this new lifestyle, like nobody's ever had wings before and those of us who do just woke up and decided to. I see my parents watch those shows, and I see them shake their blue-lit heads at night, thinking about those misled freaks and their horror-backs.

I want to tell myself that they don't know. I want to think that they're still clueless about it. But there are feathers turning up in the laundry, and my search history is full of *Am I alone?*

They keep coming to me, wan, looking like they've spent the night up researching, here to reassure me like my very own messenger angels that if I have anything to tell them, anything at all, they're right here. Like they haven't been distant.

And they go to the principal. Weekly, sometimes, just to 'have a chat'. They've spoken to every one of my teachers, one of whom paused while walking by my desk during independent study.

"Good luck, kiddo," he said, in a feather-soft voice. I pretended I hadn't heard.

My parents are spies. My parents are cold, calculating, childless, in control of an angel; loyalists to the side most opposite. They've been watching me for the signs, and when they know for sure, they'll turn me over.

extra credit.

(for rabbi greenberg.)

I saw my Jewish Studies teacher in the library. She was wearing her tichel, and she had a book in her lap with the kind of old, falling-apart covers you only saw on things written in the olden days, bound in leather. It had no title on the cover, only a painting of a flickering flame.

I guess I wasn't surprised to find out that she practiced pyromancy. It was getting pretty popular, and there were people who did it everywhere—it was a sort of fashion now, with scissor-cut skirts and black piercings to match. And now that I thought of it, perhaps my teacher *had* been walking around with a black nose stud for a while now. *I* definitely hadn't been paying attention.

But it was still weird: it was weird in the way you didn't expect your best friend to be into necromancy, or your cat to turn up after going missing for three days with a new tail. It was weird in the way that you sometimes felt when you got lost in an old bookstore, or when you looked up at the sky and saw a star you couldn't recognize. It wasn't what it used to be, and she wasn't who she was.

So I started walking. I started walking, as quickly as I could, towards the stairs at the end of the floor. I passed a magazine rack and a taped-up poster, which fell, and I looked back at it once before moving on. Going back to the stairs meant passing her chair again, with her flame-covered book, and when I got there I was struck by an impulse and paused.

Then I turned, and it wasn't my Jewish Studies teacher after all. It was another woman completely, with a long nose and a hood still pulled up on her jacket from the rain outside. When she looked at me, my heart pounded. I ran down the stairs and left without looking back.

When I went back to school on Monday, I looked a little harder at my Jewish Studies teacher. There were no piercings on her, no pyro-fashion, and nothing to prove she was studying anything out of the ordinary at all. She was just like she had always been, just like I had thought she was, and yet—I kept looking at her. I kept looking, and when she looked back at me, I could swear there was something different.

and another.

They were walking in a circle together. He came first, and then them; though if you looked at it from another angle, it was possible to interpret it the other way. Their hair was in cornrows on one side and left free on the other, and the curly floppy bit that was out was covering their eyes. He was peach-haired, and that was all.

They stopped suddenly.

He stopped just behind them.

"What is it?" he asked, and they turned to look up at him.

"I'm not getting anything," they said. Their voice was frustrated and loud in the empty room. He cocked his head, letting his glasses slip slightly down his nose, and they shrugged. "I don't think I'm clairvoyant."

"I'm sure you are," he said, in the reassuring way all parents tell their teenage children that they will succeed. He put a gentle hand on their shoulder, and they cocked their head to look up at him. There was a brief silence where they squinted up into his eyes, trying to see something there. In his all-black clothes, he looked a little like a priest blessing a child.

"I think you're going to learn your new piece," they said

eventually. He relaxed and leaned down to give them a brief hug, standing again in a moment to continue walking.

"You see?" he said. "I'm sure I will now. What a lovely piano-blessing you have given me with your words."

They looked at him sideways, examining him, but followed on behind him a moment later.

"I was only guessing," they said, and he sighed.

The circular walk continued.

cricket.

Cricket isn't bright or chirpy, but she does have a white glove on her right hand with the letters DEATH on the knuckles, and she will use it when necessary, so maybe the name's not about the insect but the sport; violence-wise. She's got a big ring of keys and a New York accent, and her speech is styled like a blunted knife.

The sign on her front door says "CRICKET'S BOUTIQUE— FOR WOMEN, MEN, AND FOLKS OF ALL KINDS," and she means it. She's got special gowns for girls who want to show off the eye in the center of their spine, suits tailor-made for three-armed tomboys, even little corsages for half-mer people who are allergic to all sorts of land plants. Yes, Cricket's is the place to go, and everyone is welcome—even humans, occasionally.

When you find yourself there for the first time, Cricket orders you to turn all the way around, first thing. Sometimes you're not even all the way through the door. And you spin quickly, very much intimidated, so she has to roll her eyes and say "*slower*," and you spin slower. Feeling like an idiot.

She shakes her head—she's got black-and-white hair, dyed all in strips, and it's distracting—like she's disappointed. You feel sort of like just backing up and walking out, like maybe this was a bad idea and you'll just go to the mall, but she squints at you and you stay put.

"Green," she says. Or maybe "Red," if that works better with your complexion. Sometimes "Orange!" though rarely. Either way, you're thrown a little further off balance, and you hurry when she beckons you over.

She takes out something completely at random (it looks like). A suit or a dress, or some other sort of formal fabric. You can see at a glance that it'll fit all your appendages, all your eyes and ears. Even your tail, if you've got one of those.

Handing the outfit to you, she thumbs you over to the changing room. It's almost invisible at first, but now you see the little booth in the back with its worn-red curtain. It's made of wood, and you're a little scared it'll fall over and reveal you halfway through taking off your jeans, but it holds.

Cricket claps her hands just as you've finished, making you start. You hurry out, and she steers you over to the mirror. You hold your folded-up clothes in your hands.

There's a mixed-up sort of reflection in it: the hangers of clothes on their portable rack, the small salon chairs in the background, several paintings of different fashion designers, and Cricket. And you.

You look good—not fine, not too formal. Cricket spins you around sort of at will, trying to get a good look at you from every angle. The mirror glints painfully where the light hits it, and you put a hand up over your eyes to shield yourself from the glare as Cricket shoves you back and forth.

You may like your outfit just like this. It's possible you won't—Cricket's not a magic-worker, after all. But she's helped all of your friends and their friends and all their parents too, so you know she knows what she's doing. Eventually, she figures you out.

And then you're standing, patient, having lost all sense of time and space, before the mirror. It reflects back a slightly different you—one with the faults ironed out, with the nerves calmed a bit. The outfit completes you. It brings out your eyes, in a way.

Cricket looks up at you, and this time she doesn't even bother asking your thoughts. She knows.

You get a few moments to yourself to look around properly—maybe you're a bit clumsy on your plant leg, or you have to see if the dress will cover your elbow-eyes at every angle. Either way, you have a lot of things to ensure, and Cricket very conveniently places herself out of the way for a few minutes. If you were to look at her—though you won't—you would find her on her phone, sending a few final messages out about adjustments, orders, different accessories to go with what's on you. You would see Cricket's foot tap quietly against her too-tall salon chair, and perhaps you'd catch her glancing at you in something harder to describe than pride or satisfaction.

When you finish, you try to figure out how to get Cricket's attention without coughing loudly or doing something similarly awkward and terrible, but she's suddenly already at your side. You lean over a little, so as not to overpower her with the lace or frills or possibly your own arms, and she measures with her fingers the random distances between cuffs and seams. This gives you a little extra time, time you didn't know you needed, to get an extra glance at yourself in the mirror. Yes, that's really you, and that *is* how your eyes look when you accent them properly.

Cricket slaps her hands together again and nods, smiling. You realize that it's the first time she's really smiled at you and find yourself smiling too, despite not necessarily being much of a smiler.

Changing out of the outfit feels like shedding skin. You may not have ever shed skin, but you loosely understand the concept now—a part of you that fit you, that was meant to cloak you, is gone. You feel very strange about your jeans, and fumble with your tail if you have one.

On your way out, you hand Cricket a prized possession—you

know what it is, you know you'll miss it; you chose it this morning in a haze of worry—and she sees you out of the shop, wishing you a good time at the dance. You wonder how she knew what style to dress you in, what level of formality to use, and how to do just that kind of thing with the thread on the edges of the sleeves, but you're already out the door, and the air is cold, and you take a deep breath of the frost as two dark-haired boys walk into the shop. You watch the smaller one bump into his brother, and consider which is here to get a new outfit.

In your head, you wish them good luck in the shop.

parent-teacher conference.

Miss Walsh is sitting at her desk, across from a parent whose name she had a bit of an embarrassing moment trying to pronounce ("Franqun—Frankin—" "Don't worry, it's phonetic"), trying to think of a way to tell him that his child is a social recluse.

"Does she talk about school at home?" This is a good opener, a safe opener. Miss Walsh likes to give parents the chance to discover strengths and weaknesses of their children on their own. She crosses her ankles under her floral-print dress and waits.

"Not really." The father has a good smile, a strong smile, and he beams it at her nonstop. There are small, deep dimples in his cheeks, and they make him look much younger than most of the other parents; she thinks he might actually *be* around five years younger than the rest.. "She talks about art, of course, and sometimes she talks about the stories you read, but everyone in our family is creative."

"Mm." Miss Walsh shuffles her papers; this isn't precisely the answer she had hoped for, though she doesn't know what that answer would have been. She turns one drawing around on the table, facing the father. "Since we're on the topic of art—she did draw this one piece that, I think, made me a little worried for her.

Many of the other children were a little scared by it."

To the father, the piece is instantly recognizable: there is a little pink stick figure on a table, a good deal of grey lightning above it, and someone with brown hair standing by it and raising their arms to the skies.

"Why, that's me!" he exclaims, tapping the brown-haired figure. "She must have picked up on my experiments. She's a clever girl; just look at these shapes..." He traces a lightning bolt, drawn with hard, definite strokes by a small hand, and watches as grey crayon slivers come off on his finger. "Children were scared?"

"Yes, a bit. I think it's—well, she's not very... social."

"Oh, I know. She likes to be alone. That runs in the family, too; at least, on my side. You know, I met Clerval in college; didn't have a single friend other than Lizzie for a very long time. You can do a lot on your own."

(Miss Walsh met both Mr. Clerval and Mrs. Lavenza at the school picnic, but is still not one hundred percent certain whether the father is dating one, married to the other, or some combination of the two with both.)

"Well, naturally," she says, "but I'm a little worried that she's not getting along well with the other children. You see, they don't really gravitate to her, and they don't... well, they don't choose her for games, or anything. I don't think I've seen someone ask her to play with them more than once, and she declined." Miss Walsh bites her lip nervously; she's suddenly afraid she's overstepped.

But the father looks just as unruffled by this as everything else; he's folding up the drawing and tucking it away into his long jacket.

"I'm sure it's fine," he says. "You know, a lot of people won't understand who you are or what you want to do with yourself. It really depends on you to get where you want to go. I'm not so concerned by whether people *like* her, really." He sighs; the first indication of anything other than joviality since she's met him. Miss Walsh leans in. "I had some problems with that myself, when I was younger—well, not so much younger. It's important to recognize and celebrate our differences, and I'm sorry I haven't always done that." He pauses. "So she's doing alright in school, then?"

"Well, yes, but the children—"

He waves his hand dismissively, then tucks a strand of hair back into his ponytail.

"I'm not so worried about the other children, as I said," he says. "I made this child, and as far as I'm concerned, she's doing wonderfully. Oh, and tell me if she falls again; I had to give her stitches—well, more stitches—after the situation with the tire swing. She's very careful, but I have a flexible work schedule, as you know, so if anything ever happens—"

"Yes, yes, Mr.—"

"Don't worry about it," he says, and walks out the door. Miss Walsh shuffles her papers, then shuffles them again. She feels, somehow, that this has all gone terribly wrong, but her ten minutes with the father are up and she doesn't have anything else she can do. She looks out the window; the children waiting for their parents seem fine on the playground.

The father's child is not on the playground; she is too cautious and too careful for that. In fact, she is hiding behind a water fountain, letting out soft giggles that echo into the hallway.

"Hm," says the father, looking around. "Now, where's my little monster...?"

The giggles louden. He walks, very slowly, to the fountain, then darts behind it.

"There she is!"

The child grins widely and stretches out her arms to be picked up. He does so carefully, avoiding the places where her skin breaks into different colors and patterns in thin little lines, but she kicks and squeals in his arms.

"What did Miss Walsh say about me?" she asks. She has a remarkable grasp on English; he wishes Miss Walsh had commented more on that.

"Well," he says, "She showed me some of your art, and I thought it was wonderful." He bounces her, and she yelps in delight. "What do you think about Miss Walsh?"

"I think she's scared of me," the child says, rather decidedly. The father raises his eyebrows. "But I like her. She's fun to play hide-and-seek with."

"Naturally," the father says, tapping the child's nose. "And you're happy at school?"

"Mhm. We all play together during tag, and last week I fell and I didn't even need to get fixed up again!"

He kisses her small, round, multi-colored cheek.

"That's my girl," he says, smoothing out her dress. "That's my beautiful, darling, creative girl."

And, holding her, he disappears among the echoes and greyness of the hallways, until he is lost in the distance.

a single cog in a very large, extremely dispassionate, stupidly proper machine.

Genevieve Beaumont-Smith locked the door once, twice, and a third time.

She was going out.

With the shop closed for the day, she headed off to the proper phone booth. Her earrings twinkled in the sunlight, and she disentangled one from the mountainous ponytail atop her head. The wind blew roughly in the salted air.

She palmed the holy rocks in one of her skirt pockets. Already, she'd planned it all: she would spend an hour or two at a cafe, drinking warm tea with cinnamon; then there would be a long walk through a small park; then she would sense out a stray cat or two and befriend them. Somehow, the city always housed stray cats. Even now, one was huddling against the wall beside her, and she guessed he'd be at the shop when she returned.

But first: the report.

She swung open the door of the booth and entered, casting a brief glance at the gum stuck to the door and the little Post-It reading *CALL ME JONATHAN* on one of the windows. It was **9:05** in the morning, and she could tell she was going to be reprimanded for not having called *exactly at 9:00!*

She dialed anyway. Not that it was much of a choice.

The phone rang only once before it was picked up.

"You're late."

The voice was crisp, annoyed, and brittle, which meant it was Jared Tenbury, and also that this wouldn't be easy. She thought she might not hate him quite so much if his accent weren't so obviously fake. Few people actually cared enough to try that hard, but of course, Tenbury was not interested in mingling with your average human.

Stupid git.

"I'm aware," she said, and added, "the sun's going to explode."

It was worth it for the five seconds of confused sputtering on the other end.

"Jared—I'm kidding."

"Tenbury, and if you *ever* do that *again*—"

"You'll fire me?"

There was a long, tangibly disgruntled pause. Genevieve was, as it happened, in a sort of mild fight with the Department at the moment. They supplied her shop, which meant they controlled her shelter and primary source of income, but *she* supplied them with reliable forecasts that they could then print in news and buyable future-packets. In a sense, each did depend on the other, but Genevieve was absolutely getting the short end of the stick—the Department could dump her at any moment, and the only reason they hadn't already was that Burke-Jones continually stepped in for Genevieve whenever there was a disagreement over her most recent transgression.

Genevieve was very, very aware that, if given a genuine chance, Tenbury would have her transferred somewhere dark and desolate within the hour.

If nothing else, it kept their relationship interesting.

"Your report, please."

They'd returned to the script. Genevieve pulled her notes from one small, change-filled pocket in her skirt and read them aloud.

"Twin moons at midnight. Four PM on a Thursday. When one dove shines. The Dragons will lose, and your tie's untucked."

"*Miss* Genevieve Beaumont-Smith—"

"Would it *kill* you to call me Jenny?"

"—your thoughts have been recorded." Pause. "Does the word 'dragons' imply the creature or the team—"

"—team, definitely, when have they ever played well—"

"—and is that prediction in any way relevant to the Department?"

She could just imagine him sitting there, phone pressed to his shoulder, pausing over his tiny little black typewriter. She'd seen Tenbury in person exactly once; when she went through the Department on her introductory (only) tour, and no less than three Recorders told her to pull her coat sleeve up because "one cannot expose one's *shoulders* in the *Department.*"

Genevieve kept herself going by remembering that Tenbury was plain-looking and unfulfilled, and she was neither, and so she was undoubtedly better off than him, somehow. She adjusted her grip on the phone and switched it to her other shoulder.

"To Burke-Jones, yes. He's going to lose a lot of money over it. Can you put him on the line?"

"Miss—"

"—Jenny—"

"—Genevieve—"

"*—Jenny—*"

"—Beaumont—"

yves.

"*JENNY,*" she yelled into the receiver, and whoever was walking their dog outside startled a bit, even though the booth was supposedly mostly soundproof.

"—Smith," Tenbury finished. "Thank you. We await your report next week at the same time."

There was a short *click,* and Tenbury was off the line. Genevieve wrestled with her thoughts briefly, then jammed the phone back onto its hook. She had every right to call back Tenbury and give him a piece of her mind, but then of course she would be *wasting the Department's time;* writing crude anonymous letters posing as various angry ministers was one thing, but openly insulting a *Recorder?*

It wasn't done.

And Genevieve wanted to keep her shop.

Genevieve slammed the booth door open and walked out, running her fingers through her hair. She looked left, then right, then left again, and upon seeing no one began the long walk down to the cafe.

don't feel guilty.

At first, the plants seemed quite innocuous, and Ephraim watched them pile up on the windows of the little greenhouse with mild curiosity. Bren had chosen to sleep in it lately; something about a new interest in plants and a general boredness of sleeping in their bedroom. Bren stood up on their tip-toes to water a few small succulents, and Ephraim smiled; there was a little bud on one of them. He had no idea where Bren had gotten six little potted plants, but as long as they were able to care for the little sprouts, it didn't seemed particularly bothersome to him.

Then Bren got more plants, and Ephraim checked in to see if they had the money to care for them. Bren insisted that, yes, they were very much able to care for the plants, and Ephraim shouldn't have worried and they didn't have to pay to get them. Ephraim had nodded, of course, and excused it.

Succulents, vines, and strawberries. Little bushes and shrubs lining the walls. Bren found green and blue and white plants and cultivated them all, and when Ephraim would come in to check, Bren would be reaching up to snip a leaf or water a pot. Every time, Ephraim looked at the different plants and felt a little less at ease.

But Bren was a teenager, and lonely, and so what if they made friends with some plants? Ephraim didn't want to get involved. Instead, he checked out books on horticulture and child psychology and did his best to make sense of the situation. He learned that most of Bren's plants were white birds of paradise, which seemed odd, given the color; and that Bren was probably just asserting their independence through caring for low-stress objects. Ephraim assumed this was partially because of his own refusal to get a cat.

Day by day, the plants grew, and the greenhouse seemed to shrink, until, entering, Ephraim found his view almost entirely obstructed by green fronds and oversized leaves. There was a large, verdant leaf pressing up against the clear windows of the greenhouse; Ephraim touched the glass on the other side. Bren's voice emanated from somewhere between the vines: "Don't worry."

Then Ephraim nodded, though they couldn't have seen him, and removed his hand. The leaf, while easily the size of his head, did not actually contain any inherently threatening qualities. Feeling slightly silly, and yet somehow still ill at ease, Ephraim backed away—and then walked quickly inside, without looking back.

He checked in on Bren a final time when the plants were beginning to threaten the roof of the greenhouse. There was a smell to them—harsh, tangy, and unnaturally bright—and it seemed to permeate through to the back end of the house. Ephraim thought some of these plants looked entirely alien; some were too green, others too pale. All seemed a little off-color.

"Bren?" Ephraim called. There was a rustling, as if Bren were turning their head. Ephraim pushed aside one large green leaf, and then another. He took one step into the greenhouse.

Deep within the obstruction of the plants, Bren cried out.

Ephraim shoved the plants aside and pushed through. Ferns, palms, caladiums were knocked away; had the greenhouse always been this large? Ephraim found himself running, and running, and later on it would seem that he had been running for much longer than was possible in such a tiny space, but now there were boughs and stems and leaves and they were endless, and Ephraim knocked them all aside, onto the ground, into the dirt; he ripped through leaves and shoots and stems until at last he finally made it to the back of the greenhouse where he found nobody; nobody there at all.

to hold a faerie court.

The goblins sat in a circle, scratching at the dirt, and She Herself held Her Own hands in Her Own lap, shining slightly. It was the beginning of a conference, and after the traditional greetings had been offered, the conversation had driven itself into nothing. Now it was time for one of them to speak, but they were each suddenly self-conscious, as if She Herself had revealed to them what they had always looked like; none moved to speak.

Eventually, She Herself was forced to ask, very quietly, if there was a particular problem. Of course there was—no one would have dared to call *She Herself* for no reason. One goblin held up a hand and, with several humble dips of the eyes, stated the overall look of the case.

One goblin had been put in charge of hiding the food—a generally useless task; given that few creatures ate the same sort of rotten things goblins did. Still, it was a ritual, and several days had passed (as usual) without incident before they had opened the badly-locked chest to find absolutely nothing. An inside job if there ever were one.

So, the narrating goblin concluded, it was now *imperative* (they had practiced that word to themself in the several hours preceding Her Own arrival), yes, imperative, to find out the truth. One of them had clearly taken the food, and would now have to pay for it (likely, in the goblin tradition, by being killed and eaten in return), but how could any of them tell who had done this terrible thing? This was why She Herself had been called.

She Herself looked at the goblin. She Herself told them they were very brave to tell the story, and they did a very goblin-flavored sort of blushing action—they turned brownish, and a little green at the tips of the ears.

Perhaps this was a more difficult task than it appeared—with goblins, it wasn't so very complex to seek out the truth, but you had to give them a good show beforehand, and if you let it drag on too short or long, someone would lose a little faith. So She Herself looked into the leaves, and then into the eyes of each goblin, and then gave Her Own answer.

It was very simple, She Herself said, to see who had committed the crime.

The goblins all leaned in, very enthusiastically. They had, of course, expected a quick and honest judgement from She Herself, but this was rather faster than had been predicted. Actually, some had put up bets (using sticks and things as currency) on the time, and none had chosen less than five minutes.

"See for yourselves," She Herself said, and she sat up ramrod-straight. "The thief's head is on fire!"

All the goblins looked at each other, but only one clapped his hands to his head.

She Herself frowned in a playfully disappointed way at the guilty party. He lowered his hands nervously.

"Selwyrook," She Herself said. "I would have expected better of you."

One goblin (perhaps slightly less shabbily dressed than the others) bowed very low, presenting She Herself with a very well-crafted sword (as goblin swords went). She Herself put a hand up to Her Own mouth in surprise, and took it very gently, as though it was the greatest honor She Herself had ever received. Behind She Herself and the presenting goblin, the others advanced on Selwyrook, and She Herself giggled softly before disappearing into the forest.

of the night.

"You got a wife?" she asked, and the synthetic smoke curled out of her lips. In the light of the city, it looked both blue and purple at once.

"Yes."

She took another drag on the electronic pipe. Its three buttons lit up when she breathed in, and the shining black of the casing reflected her pale hands in the night. This was an expensive pipe, probably. He wondered if she'd paid for it with money from her clients.

"Kids?"

"Two." He sighed and pushed his hands further into his pockets. He'd told his wife he was going to be out with some friends; the kids were probably watching their screens right now.

"Hm." The woman looked off down the nearest alleyway, then back to him. They were taking a walk; she was ready when he first handed over the money, but he was nervous. Wife and children, wife and children. It felt egotistical to assume he had needs, still, that were unsatisfied—that there were desires beyond the family, desires that couldn't ever be fulfilled.

The cars passing them by were fast and dangerous; several weeks ago, the only car dealer left had been in the newspapers for malfunctioning airbags. He'd read the story in his living room, a glass full of green wine on the table beside him. The world, he'd thought, was going entirely to shit.

So, in the long run, this couldn't be quite so bad. Rather reasonable, if you thought about it.

The Gentle-Women had only come to this city two months ago. The white-lit streets had been empty, and now no longer were. These days, it seemed as if every two blocks brought you to another glittering, smoking, lightly made-up woman on a corner. They were everywhere; those seeking them had only to look for a sequined, slightly-too-short dress.

Of course, he'd never thought *he'd* be seeking them. If his wife knew he were here—

Well, *she'd* have quite a bit to say about it, wouldn't she?

And, for its own part, the city seemed to have things to say as well. Nobody walked anymore; he was the only one out, with the Gentle-Woman, and the buildings leaned in at him ominously. There were flickering billboards and signs and neon windowpanes all up to the depths of the sky, but the air behind them was black and empty in a claustrophobic, frightening sort of way.

"You've signed the waiver," the Gentle-Woman said. He realized they'd come around to a hotel; most prohibited this sort of thing explicitly, but it was never hard to send the Gentle-Woman around a corner while you paid for the room.

"Yes," he said, and entered. The hotel had a golden roof, golden walls, and a strange gold-scented perfume. He felt slightly dizzy as he gave them his name. Had she reminded him so as to get him out of her hair? Certainly, these women now had ten clients a night. He didn't have the right to waste her time.

He exited the hotel, key in hand, and looked around. She stood up from her leaning perch against the hotel wall and stuck her pipe back into her mouth. He wasn't certain whether the smoking felt attractive or unattractive; he wondered if she'd picked it up before she'd taken this job.

The doors of the hotel opened again, and he tried to pretend that the woman with him was a guest; just someone he'd intended to bring for some other reason. A wife, perhaps.

Of course, she didn't look anything like anyone's wife.

The doormen frowned in distaste; he pressed the elevator button guiltily, fingering the key in his pocket. Technically, the hotel couldn't *discriminate*, but the services themselves were prohibited. He wondered suddenly how the Gentle-Woman would get away, afterwards, and for the first time felt bad about the possible mess.

The elevator made a bright, innocent dinging noise, and they stepped out very quickly. He led her as best he could, checking often the number on his key.

"Right," she said, taking the key from him and opening the door. She had an odd sort of accent; it made her seem rather elegant, in the wrong kind of way. She dropped the key on a bedside table and put her bag down next to it. His mouth went dry. "Get on the bed."

"Is that procedure?" he asked, and it was one-half a joke, but the look she gave him was slightly terrifying. He sat on the bed. The Gentle-Woman paused, looking at him. He looked at her. Was this how frightening it was supposed to be, or was he just with the wrong woman? He supposed there wasn't really much difference between the wrong and the right sort of woman, in this profession.

"You don't want to," she said.

"I do want to," he said. And he did, really. He was just also sort of a coward about it. The woman sighed, rolled her eyes, and returned to searching through her things. She removed several cases of lipstick, different pipes, and a single earring as he watched.

"I can send word to your wife," she said, finding what she wanted in her bag. It was black and had a silver streak down the frame. There were reports, actually, that Gentle-Women had custom ones; that they had their names written on the bottom of each. He realized that he didn't know hers, and wondered if it was important.

"That would be nice, thanks." He licked his lips, and she aimed.

typist.

Burke-Jones' hands are cramping up.

He looks at them—stops typing, holds his hands up to his face. There are blisters, and a fading bruise on the back of his left hand. Something about one of his Assignments, something about his working methods.

Rubbing his eyes, he leans back in his chair. His report, thus far, is detailed and without omission—it follows from *Clara, Seventeen, Confused and Curly-Haired* to *Janna, Twenty, Possessed* without a break. Then additional commentary—*typewriter functioning properly, e key slightly slow, mild traffic through Department, Perlman clocking out early, somewhat loud.* He realizes that he's very tired. Four pages lie beside him on his desk, and one sticks resolutely out of his typewriter. *Next appointment in,* he's written on the paper. *Next appointment in...*

He looks leftwards, leaning back further in the old wooden desk chair to see what's going on. Rows and rows and rows of typing men; all jammed together at wooden desks with black typewriters. Resolute clicking and clicking and clicking; not a pause for breath. He looks to the right, and sees the same. Above him, on large signs hung pointedly every so often along the rows of Recorders:

SOMETHING'S NOT RIGHT

OFFICIUM NOSTRUM SUMUS.

"We are our duty." Or something to that effect. He has only a passing ability to comprehend Latin; Tenbury's much more adept in that department—and look, there he is. Tenbury. Looking up over his typewriter to send a pointed glare. Burke-Jones nods, and returns to his work.

Next appointment in five minutes, he writes, and looks at his words. *Meeting with Angela; discuss...*

He pauses. It's not so much that he dislikes Angela, it's that she's *happy.* That she's very, very happy to be working like this. Calling him every week, coming to the booth at the same time, having the Department control her life. Which means he pities her, more or less. And that he can't help her.

Burke-Jones slides his hands over his face. He looks at Tenbury, who is now looking down and concentrating on a phone call. Burke-Jones can't hear much of it over the clicking of the typewriters, but he can catch enough. Tenbury's not having the time of his life with *Nielie, Eighteen, Short-Sighted and Very Stubborn.* Burke-Jones returns to his typing.

Meeting with Angela, discuss...

discuss...

yves.

discuss...

He hovers over the keyboard. He's been told to ask her about her friend; she had a horrific dream about him and can't decide if it's an omen or not. Burke-Jones isn't entirely certain how to write it down without simply stating the contents of the dream, which he does not want to do.

There's a loud clock ticking, somewhere. As long as Burke-Jones has been working here, there has been a clock ticking, and he has never seen it. All he knows of this building are the meeting rooms and the long halls, and of course this specific hall of typing men, and this is not precisely what he meant when he said he wanted to aid a cause.

Burke-Jones looks down at his typewriter and sighs.

He's about to be fired. It's not something anyone has to tell him; he knows. After Ianwen, and Jenny after her—it's not a long shot. The Department will remain as it is, and those who bite or scratch will be removed.

Burke-Jones slides one long finger down the side of his typewriter. He wonders who will receive it when he's gone. A younger man, or someone who's been here longer than him? Will it be left out, empty, until someone else comes in to fill the spot; or will somebody get it as a gift?

He is so distracted that he almost doesn't hear the phone ring.

He has a single small red phone. It is (technically) old-fashioned, with a long curly cord and a thick receiver, and it is ringing its little white rotary dial off. It is Angela, most likely, and from her Department-designated payphone, no less.

Burke-Jones looks at the phone, knowing it will not stop ringing. It has been wired that way. The other Recorders bustle around, speaking or listening into their own phones, and each clicks away at his own typewriter. Burke-Jone's phone continues to shriek, and he looks at it for a long moment.

Then he stands. He stands, pressing his fingers down against the dark wooden desk, and takes a step back. His chair is pushed slightly out of its spot, and he looks down at it. It's tilted a bit too far to the right. He takes a deep breath.

His heels click on the cool tile floor as he walks; not a head turns to watch him as he leaves.

blood-drenched brothers.

I am in the snow, drenched in blood, watching my brother die.

They said he was a monster; that he fell from the trees and grew from the ground. I never believed them, but I wouldn't have cared if it were true. He's my brother; he's as much man as me. Maybe a little more.

When we were both young, he would take me to the forest. Green leaves gave way to red, red disappeared into brown-black boughs and white-frosted branches later. With my brother, the forest was a tricksy kind of friend; one that I could trust only as far as my back was to it. I told him it was only tame when he was around, and he smiled as if he agreed.

Was he cursed? My mother thought so. She never told me why or how, but I could tell for myself that there was something wrong with the way the other people saw him. I was supposed to hate him. They told me, in their whispers, what kind of thing he was.

I grew older with him, and learned to understand, and saw why he lived in the forest. There were smaller and darker places within it, where he blended as easily as shadow met sun. His skin would flicker and peel when I wasn't looking, and suddenly he would be gone, hidden as a bough or break on a nearby tree.

We were together, always, all the same, and I never once questioned it—the way he would cock his head and change his eye color, or how he asked me to go out in the woods in the height of frost. He never needed a scarf; not even on the coldest nights.

We buried bodies together, many, after finding them in the snow, and planted lilacs over their blooming corpses. I spread dirt and leaves across the tops of the graves, rarely thinking of the light-left eyes and how similar to my brother they all looked; all pallor-skinned and earth-faced. He was *mine,* and alive, and that was all that mattered. I didn't care what the others said.

But then they came: they came, they came, *they* with their knives and pitchforks, and the forest fled as we crushed the leaves between our feet, running. It was just like it always was, he told me, just like the usual; we were running for fun, for ourselves, together through the forest, him only a little faster than me, me struggling to gain an inch here or a yard there—

He fell.

There was no sound, but the rest of the forest had no sound to it, either; it was the mob and the people that held the clamor; and all of a sudden there was a quick stab and a bullet's blast, and I bent down when they had left to see him wounded. Perhaps he had cried out; I hadn't heard.

"Ah," he said, and he said my name. I nodded, and he said my name again. "This is unfortunate."

And then he laughed, as though he could fool me—as though I didn't know what was happening to him. There was the smallest fleck of silver in the bloodshine.

I was never one for talking. I didn't have a lot to say. I sat with my legs folded and my knees under his head, and I propped him up a little. He breathed blood and closed his eyes, and the sky darkened for a moment as he tried to swallow. There was dirt under his nails, and snow stuck to his skin.

And we are here now, with the light and the dark and the forest. They, with their weapons and no virtue, have run away, but we remain. We remain, and soon I will remain. I have no flashing eyes, no self-defense, no way of hunting, not like him; but I will find them. I will find a way.

There is nothing left that I can do. My brother looks out, farther, into the darkness in the gaps between the trees, and I take his hand. He is already growing cold, even as his back, so close to the bullet, burns red-bright against my knees. I can see his eyelashes fluttering, and my breath in the air.

There are no words left, no glances, and so I bend my head and let him fade away.

SOMETHING'S NOT RIGHT

I am in the snow, drenched in blood, watching my brother die.

i know.

So Sophie lives by the woods, right? And she's looking for a hookup, right? No, shh—listen. I got ALL of this from Shaun, who's best friends with Elle, who heard from Sophie HERSELF. I know what I'm talking about, okay? Okay.

Okay, so Sophie gets her necklace. The *good* one, the one she wore to prom last night. And she gets, like, the *best* lipstick. I don't know what color; Shaun forgot by the time he got to me—but the *best* lipstick. And that means either the mauve or the green. And she gets into this dress, right, not the one she wore to prom but the one she was in at—yeah, yeah, the party in December. Mhm... *I know!* God, it was so cold, how were her legs not, like, freezing? Yeah. Oh my God, don't even... But the dress is silver, right? Silver sequins. And the *you-know-what* love shiny things.

No, they're not like—what? No. What—they're not like crows. Are you listening to me?

Good.

So she goes outside, right? In her dress and her necklace and stuff. Oh, *now* I remember; the necklace has rubies in it; must've been the mauve lipstick. Wh—because it's *important!* Look, do you want to hear this or not?

Okay, so she gets to the woods. And then she puts her *thing*—
oh my God. No. No, shut *up*—oh my God, you are so bad. No, she
puts, like, her *thing*—like her OFFERING, oh my God. Shut up.

Where was I? Oh, okay—tree. She puts it in the tree closest to
the edge of the woods, and guess what? A total *babe* walks out. No,
he wasn't human—no, that's the whole point, that's what I'm
saying. Are you kidding me? Oh my God. Anyway, this *guy*—I
don't know. I don't know, okay? She had sex with him, that's where
this is going. I don't know what the thing was; she said it looked
like a hot guy.

Anyway. The guy, it, the *you-know-what* comes out of the
woods. And it-slash-he is sexy as all shit.

Mhm.

Okay, look—it looked like Wylie, okay? It literally looked like
him. Like, that's what she said. No, you can't tell him—oh my God.
I don't care! All I'm saying is that it was like fake-Wylie came out of
the woods.

Yeah, she knows it wasn't Wylie. Because—because of course
it wasn't Wylie! Oh my God, will you let me *tell* you what
happened?

Yeah. Okay. Wylie Sanders was wandering around the woods

behind Sophie's house at one AM. Got it. Okay, sure. Are you done?

Good.

So the guy-thing comes out, and he's hot or whatever—yeah, I've never seen it either—and she's just like, oh my God. You know? Like, oh my God. And so she's like—okay, there's no way she was this badass, but like, she goes, "I know what you want." And the guy is like—you there?

Sorry. You went all quiet.

So the guy is like, "Do you?"

I know.

Told you it wasn't Wylie.

Anyway—he's like—you know what he's like, and then she's like, "Yeah. You want to—" Crap. I forgot how she said it. It was really cool, though, it was like—um—Crap. Okay, just—it was about, like, messing with humans and having fun and stuff. Just ask her. Or Shaun, yeah—no, Elle probably already forgot about it.

Okay: so she says that. And he's like—you there? Stop going quiet like that—"You're right."

I KNOW.

So she's like, something about wanting to get down, and he's like, sure—no, he didn't say "sure." I don't know what he said. He just said fine, or okay, or yes—no—Look, he was like, yeah I'll have sex with you, *that's* the point.

Mhm.

No, I don't know. What—no, I don't know what it was. That's—yeah, that's it. She had sex with an elf dude. Is this not hot enough gossip for you? You know somebody *else* who's done it with an elf dude?

Everyone has a cousin Tanya who's done it with an elf dude. That doesn't mean *shit.*

Well, yeah, sure, now she's *heard.* I mean who's *already* done it with an elf dude. Yeah, see? Sophie was totally the first. And, like, not gonna lie—I'm kind of jealous. No, I'm not dating him! Oh my God. Oh my God, you are totally making stuff up. No. Come on— okay, maybe if the thing looked *exactly* like him, but—shut up shut up shut *up!* Oh my God.

Yeah. Mhm. Yeah.

I *know.*

edie.

The night they overheard their parents planning on leaving them in the forest, Edie was thirteen and very angry. Their soft hand was pressed to the door, and they were watching an ant make its way past their bare left foot.

"...*don't have the money.*" The words filtered into a low hum through the rosewood.

"...*different... resentful?*"

"...*be like that...*"

"*necessary... very difficult... know the forest well.*"

"...*talk to me...*"

The dialogue continued behind the wall, but Edie gave up on listening. They leaned back against the door, sulking, and frowned over the dust under their desk. One lavender thread was poking out of their pajama pant leg.

'*Know the forest well.*' Edie did know the forest well. Well enough to survive in it? Why not; how else had they grown up all these years? Alone, in the woods, with the trees and their whisper-leaves for company. Sure, Edie knew the forest well.

Amidst the murmuring of the adults behind the door, there

was the clear and distinct sound of the clock ticking away the night. Vacantly, Edie gathered themself up off the floor, dusting off their sleeves and pant legs. They yawned, and climbed into bed to sleep.

The family set out early the next morning, and Edie's parents dropped pomegranate seeds as they walked. Edie wondered if they were afraid, perhaps, that Edie might follow the seeds home—not afraid enough, most likely; Edie knew the forest better than they did. Then Edie saw the paths curve, and turn, and saw their parents weave across the dirt and go deeper, and found the object of the trip.

Edie's parents sought to hide them so very deep in the forest that they would find everything around them to be unfamiliar, and harsh, and so disconcerting as to never find a way to leave. Perhaps they weren't aware of how well Edie knew the forest, or perhaps they didn't care. Edie's parents were hedging their tired, disappointed bets on being able to lose Edie in the woods while leaving a hard enough trail that they themselves wouldn't be lost. And then, of course, things would be much easier—money would appear from nowhere, the house would be happy again, they wouldn't have to bother with children... et cetera.

In many ways, it was the cruelest thing Edie had ever heard.

The trek was long, and hot, and Edie looked up at the sky

often. It was a darkish, clear blue, filled with circling crows. Edie's parents looked up as well, and worried.

When the family came to the proper place, Edie's father and mother looked at them and smiled. Edie's parents were such complacent figures; their mother was soft and round and curved in all the normal motherly ways, and their father was tall and hard and meant things in the way he walked. Both smiled at Edie, and Edie tilted their head in suspicion. Their parents did not like that.

"What's going on?" Edie asked, and their mother coughed and hid her face behind her hand. She looked left, and then right, and then straight back at Edie, and she said "Well, we'll just be a moment." Then she adjusted her shirtsleeve.

It appeared they hadn't quite planned this out.

"That's right," Edie's father said, and his face was as false as if he'd been a china doll. He smiled with shining eyes and folded his rough hands across each other. "So you stay right here."

Edie paused for a moment. They decided to give their parents a chance.

"You'll be right back?" they asked, and their voice was quiet and husked. Their parents looked surprised to find a doubt.

"Of course," their mother reassured them, and smiled. Their

father mimicked the gesture, looking profoundly alien.

"Good," Edie said, meaning nothing of relevance to the conversation. They stood, and brushed dust off of the legs of their pants. Their parents blinked. Then Edie looked up, and, very pointedly, beyond.

Edie's parents turned. There was a moment, slightly, in which they did not notice. And then they did, and were afraid.

Edie laughed. It was the first time Edie's parents had heard them laugh in years; certainly since they had begun their walks in the woods, since they had started looking for friends in the trees and leaves. Edie laughed and laughed, and their teeth were painted with burgundy seed-blossoms.

"You wanted to leave me," they said, and their eyes narrowed like black coral. Their parents realized, and startled, and licked their lips, trying to come up with the proper excuse. There wasn't any; Edie knew. "You wanted to leave me here to die."

"Wasn't quite like that—" Edie's father protested, and "So short on money—" Edie's mother tried to say, but Edie was suddenly taller, taller, taller than the two of them combined, and they stood and laughed and laughed between the trees. The odd lighting of the woods made their parents look tiny.

"Goodbye," they said, and the trees began growing together at the seams. Edie's mother and father clutched at each other, and they looked up and around, and they huddled inwards in terror, but the trees continued to grow. Up and in and out they went, and soon Edie was laughing in an empty clearing.

"Goodbye," they said again, and their voice was louder now. The forest whispered happily, licking its chops. Shrugging, Edie stuck their hands in their pockets and walked off in the direction of home.

The rushing leaves were golden in the silence.

folly.

It is a very large field, as fields go. Sort of burnt-umber orange under the wheat, and soft-blonde between it. Sometimes she can see something shift under the grass about her, and she twists to get away from it, but that is made rather difficult by the chair she is strapped to.

Tradition! Oh, the many things tradition makes us do: burn our Sunday clothes when the moon is full two nights across, sew red thread above the doorframe, put our daughters out to the field in hopes that the fae may accept them.

The trick: when something is properly tied down, the fae cannot take it. (Or her.) Not without a contract. So it is easy enough to lie and say that the ropes are for them, not the girl.

Ah, but what difference does it make, what difference does it make in the end? They cannot take her and she cannot run, and at any rate the fae may choose to ignore or adore the offering, but she is still *there,* in the heat. In the sun.

Her hair is bound just properly, below and around her ears, and the dress is not her best. Never wear your best clothes to see the fae; it offends them, and you don't want to do that—hopefully.

(Two years ago, a child was stolen. Its parents ran to the woods in a crying, shrieking rage, hatchet at the ready for whomever they might meet. Each year, it seems fewer and fewer people remember them.)

The girl is waiting.

She has gone far beyond scared. One has to, tied to a chair in the middle of a field. She is, if anything, determined. Calm, serene even, but determined. She *will* earn their favor, or... well. The fae are rather unpredictable. Perhaps the crops will fail, perhaps the barns shall burn. Perhaps a tidal wave shall come from the whispering woods. Who may know what the fae have planned?

And yet—there is a chance, a rather large one, that they will be pleased. The fae like those with earth tones; those who have brown hair or skin or eyes. Those who look as they do, as the woods themselves. The girl does—close enough that, with her hair over her rounded ears, she might be mistaken for one of Them.

Today is a frightening day, a dark one; despite the sun, not a soul leaves their doorstep. Rebellious children peek through curtains, climbing over one another for a better view. Parents hide in bedrooms and closets, waiting for the judgement to pass.

She has been told to watch the woods. The fae will only come when the field is deserted, when all the villagers but one are in their homes. She lifts her chin and steels her eyes, ready...

And look! She misses them all the same. This is how it is with Faerie: one can watch as long as one wishes, but will somehow never be able to count the precise moment the shadows in the leaves shift and change form from absence to presence, when the light itself grows wings.

They are dressed, as usual. The fae hold little respect for many human customs, but for this—for a sacrifice—they honor a single one. The girl has heard they go naked in the woods, but then, she has heard many things. She has heard they are half-animal, part-devil, all foolishness and light air. Best to appreciate the favor they show.

So she keeps her head tilted up, eyes flat against theirs. The fae of the woods do not appreciate deference: they like a headstrong character, someone who can hold their own. Eye contact is a show of power, and they enjoy it.

She looks to each of them, keeping her burned-corn eyes trained on theirs. It's the only thing the fae truly have in common: black pupils, black irises, black throughout their eyes. Their skin flies any shade of brown and green, their hair defies gravity and twines itself into intricacy as soon as the eye might move away, and they mold themselves to any clothing style imaginable—but the eyes. The eyes are always black.

The fae surround her, cover her. If anyone were looking through the curtains now—and it is certain no one would dare—they would find no way of seeing the girl through the brittle limbs. Fae touch her hair, trace one side of her jaw; she is very, *very* still.

One solitary faerie tilts its head to the right. Its tongue runs over its teeth in interest, and the girl makes eye contact. She swallows, but hopes it doesn't notice. Its eyes narrow, and she trembles slightly despite herself.

"This one." Its voice is sharp and whining, a keen sort of red-orange, high-pitched accent. The girl's eyes widen, and she keeps down a gasp. Several of the fae turn back to her face and squint at her appraisingly.

"This one?" another says, virtually indistinguishable from the rest. When the girl isn't looking at it, it fades out of her peripheral vision.

"I want this one," the first faerie asserts, and it raises its night-haired head high. The girl thinks about the stories; that the fae steal all they wear. She wonders from where *(whom)* this black leather jacket came from.

There is a cheap moment of silence, in which a bell jangles slightly on the wind. The girl forces herself to face forwards, keeping eye contact with the fae until her eyes water. She thinks her life is balanced on the edge of a string.

One faerie, then another, then another fade out of her view as they convene like foxes in a skulk. The faerie facing her tilts its head again, making the bones in its tangled hair rattle. The girl sees a finger bone there, and blinks hard to clear her eyes. The faerie smiles in a trickster sort of way.

A name floats on the wind. It's the kind one might call a bird or grey wolf, and the girl's faerie—for she has already come to think of it that way, though that is a dangerous, trusting way of thinking—answers to it in the same air-float tongue. The fae envelop the dark-haired creature, almost in a huddle, and whisper to it challengingly. Straining slightly against the ropes, the girl has almost forgotten that her gaze is no longer held.

Then, suddenly: a hand. The bone-wearing faerie's hand, and the girl takes it. She finds that her bonds are gone. The faerie's hand is warm and cool at once, cracked like wood and soft as lamb's ears, and the girl is entranced and allured. The leaves twine around her feet as she follows.

When the villagers peek out of their windows, when the children step out from the doors, there is nothing more left to see. And yet, as it may sometimes seem, many swear they catch an arm on the girl's back, leading her into the forest.

theoretical robotics and the dynamics of love.

"CC, do you feel love?"

They're on the grounds together, out in the grass beyond the Academy. Or what used to be the Academy—long ago it was taken over and repurposed to become the Envel Scientific Laboratory and Museum of Envelian Inventions. Despite Dr. Envel's continued insistence that everyone call it by its 'proper name', everyone either calls it the 'A' (for Academy) or 'E' (for Envelian, probably).

CC is one of the newer inventions in the museum; a robot who can think, speak, and act in almost the precise fashion of a human. In studying her, Envel has found only two differences between her and the average human: one, that she does not tell lies, and two, that she will not give up a moral principle.

Conveniently, these are very nice qualities to have in a person. CC spends most of her day speaking to and interacting with humans. They like her, generally. She's very polite, and she looks human enough, with her dark eyes, round nose, and slightly downturned lips. Envel built her to look as realistic as possible, with two exceptions: exposed joints, and no skin. She is a smooth, silver woman, and she is not fun to bump into in the hallway.

"I don't know skin," Envel said, when asked to comment on

CC's lack of it.

Now, the precise idea of CC's interaction with humans that she will eventually learn all there is to know of mankind and become the largest collection of human knowledge in existence. It's a bold goal, and someday she'll get there (after all, if Envel trains enough assistants, there could theoretically be an unending chain of 'doctors' to keep her healthy), but for now she is merely a large woman who enjoys learning.

Alice, coincidentally, enjoys teaching. So far she has insisted upon taking CC to restaurants serving every type of food CC can imagine, reading to CC out of books of every genre (CC does find it amusing to hear about 19th century robot-related literature), and now teaching her to make flower crowns. A silly pastime, but one with pleasant results, so CC has taken to it very well. She's glad, in her own way, that this is the caretaker who was chosen for her.

CC considers the question she has been asked, taking care to notice the "do." Not "can you feel love," but "do you feel love." Her half-finished flower crown droops in her hands.

"Can you feel love without knowing it?" she asks, first. Clarification questions are required to answer this properly.

Alice rests her chin on her hand in the grass and studies CC.

"I think you could be in love with someone without recognizing the feeling," Alice says.

CC twists another flower into her flower crown.

"Then my second question is," she says, gently picking another daisy, "what is love?"

Because the problem is that love is largely indefinable. CC has heard many definitions, ranging from "a desire to spend a long time with someone" to "a desire to do specific romantic actions with someone."

"I think it's different for everyone," Alice says. "So maybe we'll never know."

"Hm." CC rounds off her flower crown and knots it at the end.

"But I think it would be defined as a *need* for someone."

CC looks up at Alice, frowning.

"I've told you I don't require anything to exist."

"It's a different kind of need," Alice says, looking up at her. "You might not need things to survive, but you need things to have a good life. Or to really be yourself. Or to feel—whole. I don't know."

"Well, my life wouldn't be complete without the Doctor," CC

says, plopping the whole flower crown concoction onto Alice's head. "But I wouldn't say that I romantically desire him."

"Alright," Alice concedes. "Then maybe wanting someone's part of it. You want something *different* from just—friendship."

"But then what is friendship?" CC asks, now half-smiling.

"I don't know," Alice says. "I guess what we are now."

"But I don't want this to change," CC says, reaching out to place her hand on Alice's.

Alice looks down at their hands. Silver on skin.

"Was that the incorrect response to this situation?" CC asks. "It was meant to be reassuring."

Also, she just had an impulse to do it, but she's not going to say that.

"No," Alice says. "Actually, CC..."

And she kisses her.

CC anticipates it, able to pick out every action coming a mile away with her reflexes, which means it doesn't surprise her—but she *is* absolutely shocked into submission by her own lack of desire to stop it. Instead, she thinks about what she knows kissing is, what it's meant to be—and does that.

yves.

Presses back against Alice. Holds her face. Bites her lip.

And it must work, because suddenly she's on the ground and Alice is above her, on top of her, kissing her and kissing her. And CC wouldn't have stopped either, dirt be damned, grass stains be damned, if Alice hadn't—

"Oh, this is going to be impossible to clean," Alice says, sitting up. Still on top of CC. "Sorry, C."

"Don't worry about it," CC breathes. In her robot way. She feels—something. Impeding her from talking. But she's a machine, she has no *feelings*. She has no idea what this is, other than the vague snippet of a Wikipedia page on crushes and an essay on lesbianism being recalled in her mind.

Oh, no.

"Well," Alice says, wiping off her mouth gently, "lesson over for today, I guess."

And as she stands, CC can't remember if she felt whole before this, but she knows she no longer feels whole now.

So this is love.

get ready.

—slammed the closet door, locked it, and knocked several pieces of furniture up against it. She looked around, shell-shocked, and snatched Archibald up from the dresser. His black eyes widened.

"Sorry for the hurry, Archie, but it looks like I'm gonna really get it now—c'mon, buster, *into* the purse—" she smashed a little, and he squawked indignantly, hopping out to flap behind her as she ran downstairs. She had most of it—apple, keys, sharp pointy thing that was meant to go on top of a sundial—but where was the inkpot?

The door slammed open at the top of the stairs. She found her eyes watering as she searched. Archibald, apparently picking up on something for once in his life, zipped into the cupboard on the other side of the living room and began shoving open drawers with his beak. Rain drizzled down outside.

Footsteps on the stairs. Oh God, oh God; and the Department wasn't going to help with this, no, absolutely not. No rest for the witches, as they say—

Clara grabbed at the nearest drawer, praying. Ribbons, strings, assorted beetles flew out; falling onto the floor and coating her arms in rainbow debris. She rifled through them, displacing paper airplanes and crystal vials.

She almost didn't hear him coming down the stairs; books were flying out of Archibald's cupboard at unreasonable speeds. She concentrated, though, let her mind drift to two places at once, and saw both things—the man on the stairs, coming down slowly, and the inkpot hidden under ferns and alarm clocks in a pile on the nearby wardrobe. She nodded at it quickly, sending Archibald there, and then—

—blue. Blue light, blue shields, blue zips and stars of magic; her holographic shapes creating blotted patterns in the air, clicking together and apart, connecting, blocking off the room—

He stood in the doorway.

The arch was massive; it took the place of an entire wall and framed his suited figure in its white hollow. She wavered slightly; the shields flickered. He looked at the spot that had just opened, and then at her.

He wouldn't understand her if she spoke. She wouldn't have understood him, either, if he'd tried to speak with her.

Archibald smacked into her neck. The shields flickered again, and this time, the man (if he *was* one, was human enough for that) rushed—

—she held enough to give him an awful shock—

—there was a small black stain at her neck now. She jerked her head towards the carpetbag, which Archibald gladly deposited both himself and the inkpot into. Her chest rose and fell sharply. She could tell several curls were out of place.

The man looked at her. She looked at the man. The Recorders filed into the Department, and sat down at their desks to begin a productive day.

If only Burke-Jones were still there. He'd taken emergency calls, she remembered, but now he was gone—and it was just them. All the other Recorders, with their appointments and their *"it is quite simply not* done, *Miss Clara"*s. If she tilted her head properly, and squinted her eyes just so, this creature almost looked like one of them.

Clara held the blue shields, moving slowly. Her spine was rigid; she reached one arm out desperately for the bag. It hopped, sort of, in her direction, just once, and she snatched it. The shields flickered again, and this time, she let them fall.

He rushed at her, nothing holding him back. She took the bag, and she *threw* it at him—its contents spilled—for a moment he was covered in every color of flower, feather, cloth and thing—then the ink spilled, and she waved her hand.

There was a soft, quick disappearance, much the same way a figure on an old television screen would wink out. The man disappeared suddenly into a blue whisp, and then the room was empty. The Department, on the other hand, suddenly received a large, unidentified humanoid monster-creature.

Clara took a breath.

"I think that wasn't so bad," she said, and Archibald poked his nose out past the doorway. "Oh, Archie!" He squawked unhappily. "Sorry—good thing you got out of the way, though."

She held out her arm, and he hopped onto it. With a soft sigh, she looked around her room, and then the opened the front door and left. There was a distinct clarity to the sunshine.

koschei.

Mr. Sempler had a very violent death. I could see it clearly; the way the other car would slide on the rained-over streets, sharply veering toward him; the curve of the wheels skidding on the cold asphalt, sticking to and crushing leaves. He would look up, eyes wide, and the other car would hit him, and then his head would fly forward and the airbags would fail and—blood. So much blood. Glass that went through his eyes and nose and mouth. I could see all of it, and I guess it didn't bother me as much as it would have when I was younger.

A brief glance at Martha Spitzer, and I could see her quietly passing away in her sleep. She'd have grey hair by then, and would be sleeping beside her slightly-older wife (though, for now, she was still trying to date men), and the breath would leave her and she would suddenly be still. Not a drop of blood on her white-and-blue-patterned gown.

It still shocked me, sometimes, when I saw someone's death, but that was rare now. I kept my head down, nowadays. Easier to avoid the visions.

In homeroom, I only knew what three people looked like, other than Mr. Sempler: Martha, the school's most popular girl below 18; Alex, the school's most popular boy, regardless of age; and

Jeannie, who had been my friend from sixth to ninth grade. Then she'd started getting 'seriously creeped' by my talent, and we'd started drifting apart, and suddenly we just weren't friends anymore.

Which meant that I was stuck, expectedly, doing a book report with two people I'd never seen—Theresa Henries and Kitty (definitely not her real name) McMillan, who were, respectively, our grade's future valedictorian and the school goth. I had no idea what either of them looked like, but I knew I didn't want to write a book report with either.

Theresa took over most of the work, thankfully, and I didn't have to worry about doing anything more than concentrating on writing up the summary of the book. Theresa noted that I should emphasize the linguistic tendencies of the author, and I completely agreed without knowing what those were.

Unfortunately, all too aware of Kitty's personality, Theresa only assigned her the cover of our report. I had a strong suspicion that she'd seen it as a type of sacrifice; there were now mysterious symbols and deep black gashes in the paper Kitty had stolen from Mr. Sempler's printer. I wasn't even sure how she'd ripped into it like that.

It didn't really matter, though, because then she started talking to me. I'd told her that I was busy, that writing the summary was more work than she thought, and that I *did not care* about how she apparently survived on the blood of the innocents, but all to no avail.

She pestered me about her collar. She pestered me about Hell. She pestered me about the prophecy she had apparently overheard that the world would be ending, and what kind of clothing was right for that occasion, and when she might be checking back in with her prophetic friend, until I shoved back my computer and stood.

"I honestly don't care," I said, glaring at her, "and if I did, I wouldn't—"

She had no death.

I blinked.

Kitty had dark eyes, and dark hair, and skin the color of sour milk, but no death. I squinted, taking in the choppy black hair and the skull collar. There had to be something. Sometimes, after I'd seen a death a couple hundred times or so, it faded—like with my mother's lab accident or my other mom's fall. Sometimes I had to look closer.

I looked closer.

Nothing changed.

"You got something to say?" Kitty asked, and I looked at where her hands were placed on her hips. She had black nails, painted very thinly, with dirt under them. "Careful," Kitty added, and grinned with uncommonly sharp teeth. "I bite."

I looked back up at her face.

No death.

There was nothing there; nothing—no blood, no broken bones, not even a last breath. I thought maybe I just couldn't see them anymore, like some freak accident had suddenly caused me to go deathblind—

"Are you two working?"

Theresa had brown braids and wore blue overalls and was going to be hit by a car. I looked at her and watched the sedan hit her, watched her go under the wheels, watched the driver stop too late, a few feet down, get out of their car to go help her, find that it was too late; over and over and over. She raised an eyebrow at me.

"Well?"

I looked from her to Kitty, who'd just been hit with a paper ball. Kitty turned and flung it back at the person who'd thrown it; some kid who I'd never seen before but now realized had black hair

73

and glasses and a bad sickness coming to him. He flipped Kitty off, and she returned the favor, and there was still no death over her, and the guy's girlfriend was leaning on him and going to overdose on pills in two years, and her friend was going to go at 90, and when Theresa snapped at me again, her car-crash-death flashed again, and Kitty and the guy were having a back-and-forth, and I looked around the classroom to see every death I'd blocked away.

Car crash. Accident. Old age. Vampire. Cancer. Accident. Blood disease. Suicide. Old age. Suicide, suicide, suicide—

Kitty still had no cause of death.

I looked at her.

She looked at me.

I ran.

crystal and sword.

Cleare has a very small diary that he keeps on his bookshelf next to his larger books. It's leather-covered, and has a cross on the front that keeps peeling off at the edges. Sticking it down again, he opens it to the middle and finds his last entry.

The thingy is weirder than ever. I wish it would go away!!! I tried jumping into bed today and it worked—it can't get me when I'm on top of it! Wess says I should just kick it. I think he wants me to lose my leg.

The 'thingy,' as Cleare has entirely unaffectionately christened it, looks suspiciously like a small, very fuzzy dragon. But, of course, Cleare does not know that for sure, and he is not planning on getting near enough to check.

So for now, it's just an unidentified thingy.

"Are you still in here taking notes on that thing?" Wess leans on the door and sheathes his sword. "You've been doing this since I left to go practice with Immure."

"How did that go?" Cleare asks, deliberately avoiding his question.

"Fantastic," Wess mumbles. "She cornered me again."

"Mhm." Cleare's busy scribbling in his little diary again. He thinks the thingy might be larger than it looks, or poisonous, or—or—he writes down *perhaps has special powers to steal clothing??* and continues worrying.

"Look, buddy, no offense, but you're obsessed," Wess says flatly. "For the last three days, you've been—"

"What if it's laying eggs?" Cleare whispers, curling his hand in his hair. "It's scary." He pouts for a moment, then gingerly lowers his foot to poke it outside of the bed sheets. A short growl sounds from beneath the bed, and Cleare yanks his foot back to safety without a second thought.

"Cleare, *let me kill it,*" Wess says, striding over to him. "It's just a dragon, probably, and if I get under the—"

"No," Cleare interrupts. He knows Wess is trying to be the Romantic Knight Who Saves His Boyfriend, but that is simply not possible here. "I'm not going to let it eat you."

"It won't eat me," Wess mutters, frustrated, but in the end Cleare wins—as usual—and Wess agrees to just let it be for now and figure out what to do with it later. He leaves to sharpen his sword or do something else similarly soldier-like, and Cleare is left on his own to deal with the thingy.

"First things first, I need a list of ideas," he says, mostly to himself. Maybe a little to intimidate the thingy. He's going to... do something, and he's going to do it at some point, and he's going to get rid of it. *For good,* he writes in his diary, giving the words a sharp underline and three exclamation points.

Idea number 1: Let Wess fight it. Wess is pretty good at killing things; he's managed to fight Dark Knights almost entirely on his own before, and Cleare barely has to heal him these days. If the thingy is a dragon, Wess would be able to make short work of it.

Pros: He might get rid of the thingy.

Cons: The thingy might get rid of Wess.

Cleare decides against this idea and lies down on his back with his feet up in the air like a large, dead bug. He blows a strand of hair out of his face and holds the notebook to his chest.

Idea number 2: Fight it himself. He may be a cleric by trade, but one time he shot a gun and he's pretty sure he can punch things if he tries hard enough.

Pros: He might get rid of the thingy.

Cons: The thingy might get rid of Cleare.

Rolling over onto his stomach, Cleare thinks over this. How much does he really want the thingy gone? It's not so bad, after all...

Just a growly, scary, really big dark shape under the bed... Possibly murderous, but not necessarily...

Which leads him to idea number 3: Leave the thingy there forever. The pros and cons of this are fairly obvious—he'll have to deal with the thingy's existence, but at least he probably won't die. Probably.

Cleare moans a little and decides to go with idea number 2. He's going to get that thingy if it's the last thing he does... which it might be, if he's honest with himself, but that's not something that he needs to worry about, hopefully.

The next course of action is deciding what to use as a weapon. It's kind of difficult when he's on top of a bed with a thingy under it; he doesn't want to just... climb off, because then his legs might get eaten, and that would be two fewer things to fight with. Instead, he sort of springs himself a little and manages to jump off the bed, landing with a soft thump on the other side of the room.

Ow.

He sneezes shortly and gets up, brushing off his skirt. Right. Time to get rid of the thingy, hopefully once and for all. He takes a random book off the shelf—nice and heavy—and whips it directly at the thingy.

With a strange sort of roaring noise—Cleare compares it to 'a million thunderstorms and also some screaming' later—the thingy opens its maw and swallows the book.

Cleare falls back on his bottom in shock.

"What the hell was that?" Wess is back, and he's holding his sword. It doesn't look a lot sharper, but then again, Cleare doesn't understand swords to begin with.

"I think the thingy just ate my book," Cleare says, still staring wide-eyed at the space under his bed.

"It ate your book."

"Yes.

"The book that you threw at it to kill it."

"Yes."

"And now it's bigger."

"Yes."

"Okay." Wess sits down on the floor next to Cleare. "Plan B?"

"I don't want it to eat your sword," Cleare murmurs. "Or my other boo—my books!"

Cleare runs to get several books from his bookshelf. He hands one to Wess, then begins flipping through the other. He knows there are spells in here somewhere that can get rid of the thingy; he has almost one thousand of them in his whole collection. You see? Block 5 Magical Reading was *not* a waste of time. So there, Wess.

Wess opens his book at random, then closes it when the letters float around him. He pauses, takes a breath, and opens it again just to see *different* letters.

"Cleare, is this supposed to be moving?" he asks, eyes crossing as he tries to read the scrolling text.

"Ooh, sorry, you have to freeze that one." Cleare waves his hand over the book, and the text comes to a definite stop. Wess turns back to the first page and begins looking through it for ways to kill an unknown creature.

He stumbles over something eventually—An illustration of a tall wizard with what looks like a circle of light between their hands. It's not something he's experienced in (personally, he prefers sleeping through Spell-Casting), but...

"Cleare, can you do this?" he asks curiously, showing his boyfriend the page. Cleare blinks at it and nods.

"Yes, I could make a small black hole, but I don't see how that would be help—oh!" he says, understanding. And then again, in excitement—"Oh!"

yves.

"Uh, yeah, so it would eat the magic thing and explode or implode or whatever the word is—"

"—implode—" Cleare butts in helpfully.

"—right, yeah, implode, and your problem's solved," Wess finishes. Cleare looks like he might cry from happiness. "You're welcome," Wess adds.

"Thank you, Wess," Cleare whispers. He sniffles quietly and wipes at his eyes. "Okay. Okay. Let's do this."

"Do you need my help, or..." Wess watches as Cleare grabs his staff and points it commandingly under the bed.

"No, thank you," Cleare says, and he mumbles something under his breath that causes a very large, round black thing to shoot out of the staff and speed under the bed. Cleare has apparently managed to time this correctly; the thingy eats it in a matter of seconds and, with a small *pop!,* disappears.

Cleare sits down in surprise.

"It worked," he says. Wess nods, very clearly feeling a little disappointed in Cleare. Of course it would work. Why wouldn't it have worked? It was his idea.

"Yeah. I'm a genius," he says pointedly.

"Well, you're not the one who actually cast the spell, so—"

Cleare sticks out his tongue at Wess. He pauses and smiles, little dimples appearing in his round cheeks. "But—thank you."

"Right. You're welcome," Wess says, shrugging. "So, now that finals are over and your bed's not haunted, do you want to go out or something? Parry found a new ice cream shop yesterday."

"Hm." Cleare taps his chin. "I might have things to do."

He looks around the room, and he and Wess both note the incredible amount of mess lying around. Cleare hasn't really had the opportunity to dust in a while. Wess sighs and leans his sword against a bookshelf, then stands to stretch.

"Okay," he says. "I'll help you clean."

Cleare jumps up instantly and kisses Wess's cheek, taking both of his hands. Wess leans forward and rests his chin on Cleare's head.

"I'm glad you're alive," Cleare says sweetly.

"Yeah, me too."

the butcher.

There were lilacs, soft and tall, in the dirt behind the butcher's shop. Their stems were curved, a sort of sickly green, and if anyone had noticed them, that person might have wondered who had planted the flowers in such a strange location; for behind the butcher's shop was nothing, not a single building, all the way down to the marsh.

In the night, there was a sharp glint to the few stars one could see; despite the fresh air and clear skies, something kept the light hidden. It was, some said, in the merit of certain sinners who lived in the town. Over time, people had begun taking that to be the truth.

Ava slammed the knife down and split the meat in two.

One small part laid by her left hand; red, and bleeding slightly. The greater part remained to be divided, and so she laid the knife carefully down, with the sharp side cutting ever so slightly into the cow-flesh, to measure out the rest of her cuts before she continued. Then her knife flashed, flew, and was still, and she put the pieces in a small paper bag.

The bloodstained apron was white across her wide chest. It tied up in the back, with a bloodied white bow, and reached down almost to Ava's thick boots. She washed her hands often, and when they were clean and pure and dark in the filtered light of the shop, she would start again on her cutting and slicing and dividing meat.

The bell rang: she had a customer. A woman from down the street, with a request for ham. Ava looked at her pinched, pale face and saw that she had a family, most likely a husband and one or two children. She would take the meat home and prepare it herself, and there would be small green leaves outlining it on the clean white plate. Some of the flowery patterning of the dish would show, and perhaps the juice of the meat would stain it temporarily; the pink flowers would turn red-brown. The children, freshly scrubbed and pink-cheeked, would lick their lips—there would be a light in the husband's eyes.

Ava wrapped the meat silently. It was very rare for her customers to make small talk with her, which was, for the most part, how she liked it. She wasn't sure she had anything to say.

The woman left, and as the bell rang again, Ava had a vague memory—one of the two young girls who had come to get meat for their individual families, on their first visit to her. It was common to send girls to the butcher only when they were already nearing marrying-age; most of the children stayed away, or were kept away by their parents. Perhaps being sent to Ava was like a rite of passage. At any rate, she wouldn't have been told.

The girls had stood, gossiping quietly, and Ava had pretended she couldn't hear as she found them the right cuts and wrapped them. The money had clinked in their hands; all golden light and noise as they shuffled it across their fingers and palms. The curve of their dark hair had glinted in the morning light.

When Ava handed them the meat, they had thanked her in a sort of perfunctory way and left, and one had whispered to the other about how Ava was, in fact, very pretty... What a pity it was that *no one loves the butcher.*

It was not the first time Ava had heard the saying. It was a popular one, and generally not used with any relation to butchers. It was about certain types of undesirable people, and generally used when speaking on someone who seemed intensely unlikable. It only *came* from butchers, really. Ava looked down at her bloodstained apron and touched it with a clean finger. Nothing came off on her hand; the blood was dry. She rubbed at the fabric uselessly.

When the night fell, the moon came out in its fabric of unseen stars. There was a soft rustling wind through the grass; a wind that tasted of dust and hiddenness. Ava stepped out of her shop, bag in hand, onto soft dew. The lilacs fluttered slightly, then were still.

The night walk was brief, and took Ava only slightly further out into the open air. It was a half-a-mile walk to the marsh, and she halved that and stood in a silent, secluded place that was as cold as it was wide. The night spread around her, and she waited for the very pit of darkness to arrive.

A shadow appeared, on the edge of the marsh. It was dark and shaped like an almost-human, and trailed bits of pond scum and leaves as it walked. Its shadow-legs were wet and slick, and should have caught the light, but remained dark as the night itself as it moved. Upon appearing before Ava, the monster did not appear any lighter. She was a reflection of the innermost depths of the swamp.

Many would have been afraid. Many *had* been afraid, back when the disappearances were common and the men still went into the marsh. Their long, explorative ventures into the darkness always ended in nothing; in a darkness that went deeper than death and colder than the abyss of fear itself.

Ava held out her bag. The meat inside it was raw, and was starting to smell slightly. She watched as the monster held out a hand, almost tentatively, and as the monster's fingers curled over the top of the brown paper. The monster had long fingers; long *nails,* too, and her hands were wet and cold. They dripped faint water onto Ava's hands, which stilled themselves so as not to shake.

The exchange was silent, and the monster regarded Ava with

dark, swirling eyes. The clear lids came down over them, slowly, and suddenly the white highlight on the wet black eyes shivered. The monster had long, dark lips, and she licked them silently.

Ava raised her empty hands, intending something. She had been intending it for a while, in fact. Simple signs. A confession. She knew the monster would understand, understood, despite having never tried to speak to her. Still, Ava's hands were silent.

The monster waited a moment longer, but when Ava did not move, she looked up into the sky. A summer storm was gathering there. With a quiet, strange glance back at Ava, she turned and began to stalk off towards the far-off trees again; slowly melting, with her unsteady gait, into another shadow.

Ava stood in the grass, with the raindrops beginning to fall around her, and her hands were still. In a moment, it became impossible to tell the rain apart from tears.

gold-based offerings.

I'm perched on the edge of the fountain, but I'm still invisible.

New people come to throw their coins into the fountain every day, but nobody's ever noticed me, and nobody will ever know that this is the one place where wishes really come true.

There's a little girl holding a dime in her hands, and I watch her grubby fingers curl around it. When it hits the water, I shake myself out a little and consider—*should* I give her a pony? In many ways, that does seem a bit much.

Then again, I am the green-haired god of the Sylvie Place Fountain, so who am I to judge what too much is.

I create a new horseback-riding camp somewhere off in the woods and send a flyer down to her mailbox. Her parents will see it, and she'll get her pony; possibly less unreasonably than she might have wanted, but still. Pony delivered, and wish very much granted.

You know, I didn't *ask* to be this god. I could have become god of the last ungoverned quarter of the Pacific Sea, or perhaps the god of lost children, or the god of fireflies or sewing needles or mended shoes, but I got stuck with Sylvie Place Fountain.

I step into the fountain and pick up a penny. This is probably the only upside to godhood: no one truly sees me. They might notice me for a second, or think that what I'm doing is odd, but they'll forget before they've even turned away. Nobody will ever report me to the authorities or even say hello.

Because I'm not allowed to talk to them. I'm not allowed to touch them, or speak to them, or show myself at all. I'm not allowed to reveal the magic behind the act. That much has always been clear, and that much is assured—I'm the behind-the-scenes god, who will never be really known. Sucks to be me.

And then there's rule two to godhood: No leaving your turf. And this works fine for Zeus and Poseidon, of course, because those guys are rocking Earth-long territories, but when it comes to me, I'm stuck to a couple hundred feet around a stone fountain. Not very glamorous.

So I stay here. Every day. Granting wishes. And sometimes, I let myself dream about what life could be like beyond the endless problem-solving of how to grant dreams. And obviously sometimes I do like granting wishes—I like making people happy. I like brightening people's days. And, okay, sometimes it's nice to not be seen. Even if that's not something I control.

Man, do I hate and love my job.

Speaking of love (not hate! Forget I said that)—Blondie. Not his real name, of course, but he's so blonde I keep forgetting. He looks like a little bunny. Not that I've ever seen a *real* bunny; people don't carry those around in malls very often, but of course I've seen Easter ads. Bunny-blonde.

And this guy—he comes so often. I know it's because he's some kind of soap addict (buying soap on his birthday? Getting more lotion because he ran out in a week? Looking for bath bombs on Labor Day? I mean, as a god I know I have naturally flawless skin, but *what?),* but he drops a coin in the fountain each time. He's one of the few guys I've seen at my fountain ever, and probably the only one who's returned. Definitely the only one who's returned multiple times.

So of course he's my favorite.

(Is it true humans pretend they don't play favorites? I've heard it's morally wrong—but I'm a god, so of course I wouldn't know. Blondie is my favorite, either way.)

Every few days or so, Blondie comes by and drops a coin in. The routine doesn't change too often—he wants a new soap, or more money, or just your good old best-day-of-my-life wish. I like people who wish for the best days of their lives—they know what they're doing. I don't get payment of any kind for being a god (what do you think, I'm gonna go buy myself some jeans with the offering money?), but some of these wishers are innocent enough that I don't mind.

Blondie asks for a scented candle this time, and hey, who am I to decline? Sure. He'll get a brand new, strawberry-and-lemon scented candle at the office Secret Santa in a couple weeks. I've got no problem with that.

Wrapping his scarf a little tighter around himself—it doesn't snow around here, but it gets pretty damn nippy this time of year— he walks off to his soap shop.

I kind of watch him for a bit, because I do like him, but I'm also feeling a lot of things. Comes with the job, I guess. Maybe it's not different from any other time I see this guy, but... I want to wave. I want to yell. You know, say hi, talk, introduce myself. Not even as a god, just as some-guy-who-likes-your-hair. Be normal for once; look at someone and have them see me, too.

It's really dumb, but I wish I could be the one to hand him his scented candle. Personally, with a cute little tag and all.

Sucks to be a god.

And, of course, a couple weeks later, Blondie is back. I watch him make his wish, and when he leans over, I flip a coin out of the fountain. It's cheating, I think, and I probably shouldn't be able to do that, but I can. Maybe because it's just out of his vision. He's not really *seeing* me.

Blondie finishes his little wishing moment (to find that quarter he lost last week—it's right in his jeans pocket; he'll find it as soon as he steps into the store) and looks down, and hey! Happy face! He looks around, like someone's going to stop him, and then just picks up the penny off the fountain's side.

"Lucky penny," he muses, and hey, is that not just the cutest thing you've ever heard?

I grin at him, though of course he can't see me, and when he straightens up again, I almost topple over before remembering to move back. I don't think humans can feel me—I tried a couple years back, and I just passed right through—but you've got no idea what it's like to have someone pass through your head. Unless you're a god, too, in which case does that not *suck?* Oh my God.

(Ha.)

He looks around a bit, into the fountain and outside of it, and gives the whole thing a really weird look before leaving.

Which is kind of strange, I guess.

The next time he returns, he walks all around the fountain first. I walk around with him, even though he can't see me, and keep myself one step to the left; just on the stone border. The mergoyle—REALLY ugly statue, sits in the fountain, sprays water everywhere—spits at me.

When Blondie stops his circular constitutional, he kneels down. Right at the edge of the fountain, like he's praying. And I have to say, it feels pretty good to be prayed to like a regular old god. Sylvie Place doesn't get a whole lot of pagans.

I'm so busy with my little godly moment that I almost don't notice Blondie taking out a quarter.

I would really, really like a kiss, he thinks, and flips the coin into the fountain.

Oh.

Oh, okay.

Well, that's definitely a wish. And I can't back down on a wish, right? Sworn to grant all. Mostly against my will, but—well. I have to. I've got to. And this is a wish, and a normal one, and I should just grant it already instead of twirling in thought-circles.

But first: a way to get out of the inevitable.

Did he specify kiss on the lips? Is his mother nearby? Can I find a stranger—any way to keep it from meaning something?

Why am I so opposed to him getting one measly kiss?!

SOMETHING'S NOT RIGHT

Okay. Omniscient. I know why. But that doesn't make it any better.

Look: it's been a while, okay? A while of me granting wishes. And I'm not saying I deserve a *kiss* for it, but... Something. I deserve something, don't I? A bit of brand recognition? Bragging rights? Something? Maybe I just *want* a kiss, even if I don't deserve it?

And he's standing there now, looking into the fountain, so I figure I'd better figure something out fast. He looks kind of like he wants to do something, or say something, but I've seen a couple hundred people do that before walking away (everyone's an atheist nowadays) and thinking about his next move for him isn't going to get anything done.

Maybe I can have one of his dogs kiss him? Maybe I can have one of his aunts kiss him. Maybe I can work something out so that he kisses someone at a bar, or a kissing booth, or, or...

Or maybe I'll wait until he finishes fishing out another quarter to decide. I have a bit of time before this wish starts seriously eating at me; I can decide in a minute. Also, I'm just really curious about the guy who's apparently looking to ask for *two* wishes today.

Blondie looks this one over for a while, and I'm tempted to read his mind. I know I shouldn't; it's probably impolite, and the last time I overheard thoughts I just got depressed (do you humans have no idea how to *communicate* with each other?) so I stay out. For a little while.

And then I skim over the top, just like sticking a toe in the fountain-water, and I'm pretty proud of Blondie, because—he gets it. A little. He's figured it out; something's up with this fountain. I don't think he *knows* knows, but he knows just a little. Enough to believe in magic. And now I *really* want to kiss him.

I almost miss him tossing the coin into the fountain.

I want to know what's behind this, he thinks, and I'm insulted for a half-second (*what?* I'm a *who,* you rabbit-haired scarf-wearer, I'm a *god)* before I actually catch on to what he just said. Thought. Wished. Because the quarter's in the fountain, which makes this an official wish, and now I've got to grant it. I think. Somehow?

...Is this even allowed? Can I even do this? Is it legal for me to show myself? Is it *possible?*

I'm pretty busy trying not to show myself and also show myself to him, and puzzling over whether I can (physically, spiritually, morally, and ethically) and I kind of fall over myself on the fountain (it's *slippery,* alright?) Next thing I know, I'm on top of Blondie.

The scarf's pretty soft. He's pretty solid. There's nothing in the fountain that feels like this.

And I'm being stared at. Whoops. I clamber off of him, which sort of works out okay, but he still looks kind of in shock, which I guess is justified. He's cute when he's surprised.

"Sorry," he says, and his voice is all soft and light, and I didn't expect that, but I guess I should have because what other kind of voice would he have? It's just weird because I've only ever heard his thoughts, and those are always in *my* voice. But okay.

"Don't worry about it," I hear myself say, and it's amazing to really *talk* to someone. He looks at me so hard, like he's trying to see through me. And that's when I remember his wish, sort of nudging at me from behind. I can feel it getting a little irritated that I haven't actually granted it, but hey, I've been busy getting *corporeal* here, and—hey. Hey! "Actually—I've got something to give you."

the hands and the mouth.

The boy runs into the market, stops, looks around. Before he even sees me, I can feel how his eyes will catch and stick. Then there's his panicked jog, flowing sleeves tucked into his sides, and the twisting of a large gold ring around his hands as he catches his breath, waiting to speak to me.

You get all kinds in New Riesia. Foreigners, natives—everybody's different enough to be the same here, which means I have no idea where this kid could have come from. He might have lived here sixteen years, or maybe he's just gotten off the balloon. Either way, he looks like he's going to trust me, and all because we happen to have the same arrangement—two eyes, two ears, one nose, one mouth, and four appendages. Skin, too; we share that in common, unlike the mechs that are entering the marketplace, swinging their salt-iron heads left and right.

Oh, shit.

The mechs are for him.

He swallows, and in another moment, speaks:

"He doesn't have much time. Soon they will see him again, and take him away. Rosauro imagines a cage; a small, dark cage, where they will put things like him. Special things, that they can look at

and laugh over and keep forever in their masters' houses. ROSAURO (panicked): I need somewhere to hide. Please."

My mouth drops open.

He stares at me, and adds, *"ROSAURO: I'm trying to find my way. Can you help me?"*

Of course I can help him. I've lived here all my life; I have three different hidey-holes, places I live in that I've taken over or dug out, in three different corners of the city. Things like that require watching, waiting, getting to know everybody, doing those little things that make everyone like you, that get you money—and knowing where you are. Always.

The mechs' spinning, silver-blue eyes lock onto him. There's a whirring sound, and the crowd around us begins to dissipate, not wanting to get in the way of the mess. The guy—Rosauro?—looks behind himself, then grabs onto my arm.

"ROSAURO (pleading, desperate): Please!"

I grab his hand, and run.

He's a lucky guy. He could have easily picked some humanoid who didn't know more of the city than the Core, but nope, he got me—someone who runs, someone who can think, in half a second, of six different places we can hide in, and then just as fast find the best one. Someone who still knows enough to keep your mouth shut and sign if you want to get your way, in Common, like a normal person. I yank Rosauro's arm and pull him down an alleyway, something the mechs are too thick to get into. They could send for dogs, of course, and try to smell us out that way, mechanically speaking, but that would take too long, and what they want—

Well, I guess I don't know what they want. But I assume it involves him, and the way he talks.

I yank Rosauro's arm and point upwards, where a series of carved footholds (made by Aito, three years ago; nice guy, hired me to fix his fence) lead up right to the buildings' roofs. Aito won't be around, not anymore, and we can use his system—I shove Rosauro up onto the first steps and follow close behind. The mechs surround the building; I wonder if these can climb without handholds; the old models couldn't. I haven't worked on any of them since the new camera updates happened, something like a year ago.

The mechs are big, and dumb, but not bad for their jobs. They're fast and intimidating, and pretty much anyone who looks into their tall metal faces yields pretty fast. Which means they're probably not after Rosauro's rings, or his pretty clothing either. I'm guessing that they're after him.

SOMETHING'S NOT RIGHT

Stupid kid, I want to tell him. Opening your mouth like that.

I thought all of the story-speakers were gone. Stuff about them used to be on the TVs; big talk show panels about whether we should shoot them or drive them into tiny holes in the ground, and always ending with that same old question—*Why can't they just talk normal?*

In a world of creatures with four eyes and seventy tongues, someone's still bound to get the shaft.

Rosauro has no upper body strength; he clambers over onto the top of the roof just barely fast enough to keep the mechs from reaching him, they're climbing up the sides using windows as footholds and God *damn* it I forgot they could do that; I grab Rosauro's arm and run. He follows me, jumping from roof to roof, gasping all the way. I have to pull him on by the fourth; the mechs are still behind us and they're going to keep following. I tug on Rosauro's sleeve—fine, soft material, something he probably made himself—and slip into a window. It takes a moment, just a moment, for him to follow me, dropping clumsily onto the floor, and then we're standing in someone's bathroom.

We run through the house, knocking over tables and triangular TVs, until we make it to another window, where we can switch houses, and then (thank God) a *slide,* one of those real old-fashioned cold stone things that leads out back to the paths by the canals, right up from the roofs—

"Rosauro has lived here for years now, hiding from the people who want to hurt him, but he has never been this far from the Core. He is lost, desperately so, and he is afraid that the other boy is going to lead him somewhere far worse than even the mechs' cages. He thinks—"

I clap a hand over his mouth, because *Shut. Up.* His eyes widen; I remove my hand. I feel awful.

Then I push him down the slide.

He screams *(bad idea bad idea)* and I move to go after him immediately—

There is a mech at the bottom, waiting. It is tall, spidery, human in its odd-jointed limbs, and it grabs Rosauro, who beats at it with his short, beringed fingers. I can't believe he's lived here *at all* and not learned to fight a mech, but then I realize that he's actually going to lose, he's only aiming for the eyes, and the thing's much hardier in the face—

I grab a lamp and slide down, stopping myself with one hand to swing and *smash* the damn thing in the neck, where the wires are most fragile. It falls, and Rosauro falls with it, tumbling into the water.

"ROSAURO: Help!"

I dive in without thinking, grabbing him. Again: lived here for years now, doesn't know how to swim? Doesn't know where to hit a mech? Doesn't know how to navigate past the *Core?* I hold onto the bank, trying to reorient myself, and Rosauro clings to me. He's warm, but shivering; I wonder whether he's as young as he seems. He's my height, isn't he? He might even be older.

Mostly, I am thinking that the last time I saw one of the story-speakers, they were getting shot in Jiny Square. TV debates going too slowly, I guess.

"ROSAURO (quietly): Please..."

I manage to haul him up onto the bank, slipping off slightly myself, and I barely manage to grab a piece of the bank on the way back. No land here; it's all hard-packed stones and golden pebbles.

I heave myself up, and Rosauro even offers me his hand, though he's so light it doesn't feel like he's doing anything. He looks at me for a moment, brows turned up in fear, and his lips part. I don't know how to keep him from talking; I don't think there is a way. And then, beyond the instinct, I get the feeling that I want to know what he's going to say.

yves.

"ROSAURO:," he says, and I hold onto his shoulders. I need to know. *"Thank you."*

I look at him, my eyes darting across his face, taking it all in— bronze skin, irascibly long curls, big dark eyes. I almost open my own mouth.

Then the mechs return, over the body of their dead friend, and Rosauro smacks into me, terrified. We're not going to be able to disable them all—hell, I don't know the last time I met anyone near tall enough to reach their necks to begin with. Kanso made his stilts, yeah, but that was almost seven years ago, when I wasn't old enough to drive a dinghy—

Now it's Rosauro who takes my hand, and we run again. I lead him in and out of alleyways, sidewalks, across roads and down to another place where two canals meet, where my apartment is, where nobody can get to but us. I tug on his arm, and he follows me onto the cliff edge.

They didn't build a bank here. Not really. They just let the water rush down, down, down, and so what might have become a bank became a narrow strip of stone, just on the outer layer of the thick Core announcement pillars. Rosauro closes his eyes, and sways slightly.

"He has always been afraid of heights... Ever since he was a

little boy..."

I reach out, and Rosauro gives me his hand. This one has only one ring, I notice; silver, with an inscription. I can't read it from here, but I feel now the metal against my skin as I walk out onto the ledge.

We have to go one foot at a time.

I don't look behind me—*that* would mean falling for sure, looking anywhere but ahead would mean falling—but I can hear Rosauro's high, frightened sounds. The water rushes below us, hitting scrap metal and shattering across the rocks, and I squeeze Rosauro's hand to make him feel safer. When we reach the hole, the place I carved into the back of the pillar, I hear Rosauro sigh, and he almost wobbles, but I hold on. He rubs the back of my hand with his thumb, and I almost fall in then, too.

But we make it. Little by little, we make it. I head in first, ducking, and then Rosauro follows. There's a little rug, and a table, and benches along both the right and left wall—no, I couldn't be assed to carve the walls all the way back, so those are benches now—and I lead him to the left wall's bench. It's probably more solid.

"He looks around, shocked by what he finds. He pays for his apartment from his weaving, but this is something someone built—

something the other boy, he realizes, must have built. He has so many questions; he can't figure out the right one to ask first. ROSAURO:" he says, and I'm waiting. I'm waiting this time, I'm ready. Nobody knows about my apartment, and the mechs won't be able to climb the ledge—no footholds large enough, no windows here. *"...You saved me."*

I look at him—just look at him, really look at him. I realize since he first spoke to me in the market, I haven't had a single second of trying to hide myself from him. I don't know how long it's been since I've let somebody take notice of me.

Our eyes meet.

Rosauro's lips part gently.

"A beat," he says, so quietly I almost don't catch it. Then I smile. Rosauro waits, but I don't open my mouth, and then he looks worried again.

"ROSAURO: Nobody should be afraid to speak." Rosauro's lips turn up into a sweet grin. *"(abashedly) I write, to give the orders. To pay the rent. But still I think—"* He stops, nervous. *"I'm sorry. I don't know if—you can't talk—"*

I shake my head. *There's a difference between* can't *and* don't talk, I think. I almost say. My mouth is dry. I meet Rosauro's fingers, curled into fists, across the table, and he unfurls them slowly so that we can hold hands again.

"He remembers his rings. He hopes they're not uncomfortable, in fact, he moves—" Rosauro begins to take his hands away, but I pull them back, shaking my head. Rosauro smiles, but his eyes stay sad. *"...he doesn't even know the other boy's name."*

Talk. Talk. Talk. Talk. The command echoes in my head, bouncing around, and I try to make it stick. I have to do it. I have to talk. It's okay, it's okay, I can talk now—if I *can* talk, maybe he's right, maybe it's been so long I won't be *able* to talk, and I think that would be the worst thing of all. I open my mouth. Rosauro squeezes my hands encouragingly, and then I hear my own voice again, slightly hoarse, and I say:

"It has been so long since Graecen has met someone like him."

soliloquy.

God made the Solitaries first. Then, disgusted by us, he created humans, sending his only accidents to live in the sewers and cemeteries of society.

Or so the story goes.

But we Solitaries *did* come first. We were the first, and we will be the last, and we are perfect.

Each hand, arm, thigh, ear—all are equally useful. All are equally free of blemishes. We do not have any need for body parts which rot, or burst, or otherwise render themselves unusable or dangerous (what on *earth* an appendix is for, I will never understand) and, unlike humans—who have been evolving and changing and attempting to reach the standard of perfection they will never achieve for millennia—we are already there. We are the destination. All of humanity is rendered useless by our existence.

And yet: we are shunned. Something about us is frightening— we are neither alive nor dead, breathing nor rotting, eating nor sleeping. Perhaps perfection is its own kind of horror.

When my mother showed me a human for the first time, I was full-grown and already quite feral enough. She and I were equal in height and size and stature, and she was only my mother in name, for there is no creation or end to a Solitarie—we simply *are,* and then we *aren't.* Like a candle flame.

I watched the woman from under a tree, and I saw everything unreasonable and odd about her. Strange colors applied to her face, uncomfortable shoes on her feet, and an umbrella with entirely unnecessary spots—white ones, on a yellow background.

She was very unforgivably human, and I was very unendingly curious.

My mother was not—human or curious. She saw humans as ridiculous to the point of being impossible to understand and wisely advised me not to bother.

Fortunately, I did not have to obey.

I therefore set myself to watching the woman for a trial period of several days, absorbing as much information as possible from passing humans and several books I found in a library—the only human invention of any use; despite having an abnormally large fantasy section. Why read, I wondered, if not to learn? Why spend your time in worlds that did not exist?

I was frustrated that I did not understand the human race, and resolved myself to the task of deciphering it.

**

When I appeared at the woman's apartment door, she was very confused.

"I think you have the wrong apartment," she said, and she was quiet and unsmiling, and I said, "I would like to ask you a question," and she frowned.

I was not pleased with the beginning to this conversation.

"Why do you have a yellow umbrella with white spots on it?" I asked, and she looked up at me in mild confusion.

"My sister gave it to me," she said. "To borrow. I don't know where she got it."

"Why," I emphasized. Her face cleared.

"Oh. I don't know."

I stayed on her doorstep, waiting for her to figure it out. She did not seem to be making efforts to do so, and so I stared down at her to prompt her. Humans are, among other things, easily intimidated by taller creatures, so this was meant to be quickly accomplished. I have not measured myself, but I am certainly taller than any human.

The woman opened her door a little wider, walked down the hall into a different room, and took something fluffy and pink out. She handed it to me, and I looked at it.

"You're all wet." Her voice was very soft. I looked up at her, and she pointed at the fluffy pink thing. A fur? "Don't worry, I have other towels."

Towels.

Books had mentioned towels, but I had not properly understood their physical shape.

At any rate, I put this one on my head, and then put it on another part of my head, and then touched my forehead with it. It was very absorbent, but I had too much hair for it to properly take care of the matter of my being wet.

"Come on in, I'm making tea."

The woman had managed to steer herself into a kitchen, or perhaps a dining room; whichever it was that one might use for making tea. I knew what tea was, at the very least. Though it wasn't as though I was planning on drinking it.

In the woman's house, among many rugs (the floor was carpeted, why did she need them), and many plants (they took up space, why did she need them), lay stacks and stacks of thick white canvas (*why did she need them*). I stepped over to one, picking it up to inspect it, and found it entirely untouched. The others seemed identical, though differently sized.

"Oh! My paintings." The woman abandoned her kettle to rummage through the squares and rectangles, and suddenly appeared with an over-large portrait of another human.

More questions: why on earth might one want another human in the house? And why, if one *did* feel invested in the idea of living with more humans, would one need a non-living variant? Certainly, Solitaries did not often interact with humans, and most seemed happily ignorant of us, but cheap imitations were absolutely not necessary.

"What do you think?" she asked, and I gave her my honest opinion.

"I am confused by it."

Her eyes wrinkled at the edges when she smiled—another reminder of her finite life and strangely-proportioned body.

"What's so confusing?"

I looked at her and then at the painting. It seemed so obvious.

"It is a copy," I said. "Of a human."

"Yes." The kettle whistled in the background, and she ran to pour the tea. I followed her, taking a seat at her round, needlessly large table. It looked as though she might be able to seat six, and yet—I looked into the hall. One bedroom.

SOMETHING'S NOT RIGHT

Of course I would find the only human who existed in solitary while doing everything possible to change that.

She paused for a moment before handing me the tea, and I thanked her—another odd human ritual. Looking around herself, she took in the mess for what appeared to be the first time. I gently pushed my tea away with one finger.

"I *have* been looking for an assistant as of late," she said, flapping her arms absentmindedly against her apron. "I don't suppose—" And then she broke off, and looked at me, and I made a decision in the perfect amount of time.

"I would be happy to help," I said, and it was my first lie—but I already understood why lying was necessary. I thought that a longer stay might, perhaps, yield further clarity.

The woman nodded and went to sit down at her table again, tucking a dark coil of hair behind one ear. I watched her contemplate the pattern in her tablecloth for a moment before lifting her teacup to her lips, and set myself to the task of pretending to take a drink.

**

On the first day of my apprenticeship to the woman, I began washing brushes.

yves.

It was easy enough to pass off my knowledge of these things as previous experience; in fact, it was simply an obvious task. The woman attempted to show me how not to bend the bristles or get paint caught higher up, slowly bringing the brush end back across her hand, and I waited patiently. She seemed so intent; so unaware of the needless dragging-on of her every action.

Her arms moved with direct purpose when she painted. She kept her movements drawn out; lengthened. Every stroke required a pause, a thought, a tracing movement in the air above the canvas, and then finally the quiet and intense motion of the brush. I finished my work more quickly so as to watch the blocks of color come together.

When I moved to leave hours later, the painting was not yet finished. She tilted her head one way, then another, and then she stepped back and squinted. I watched her sigh, stretch, and put down her tools. Her hands, in the process of her work, had become mottled and dirtied in a most colorfully excited way, and I watched again as she slowly, uselessly ran a wipe over them which removed only the topmost layers of pigment.

**

The second day was brighter than the last, and warmer. The woman opened a window, letting in a fluttering breeze that combed back her thin dress and toyed with her hair. She batted at the curtains, stretching one hand back to comb through her ponytail as the other reached for a watering can. She dropped the can almost instantly, persistent as she was in doing two things at once.

Today her painting seemed to trouble her. She used her hands more than once, smoothing down different corners and touches of paint. At certain points, she stood up and took a break from the painting entirely; seeming to lose interest and find it again seconds after playing a match of some kind of game against herself. I glanced over at the board afterward (given the messiness of her apartment, I assumed it would also be my task to tidy it for her) and found only a rash of red-and-black squares and some odd round pieces.

When I finished cleaning, I simply stood, watching her. I found that the painting's unfinished state was not an accident but part of her work; despite her speed in bringing color to the canvas, the layers of paint took hours to come together and make forms. She was both fast and slow, and paused often to step back and look at her painting from another angle. Many times, she was forced to correct mistakes.

During her next break, she was surprised to find that I had cleaned her 'checkers' (as she called them). I pointed out that she was not using them, and she said she supposed that was fair enough.

Instead, she took a moment to show me the reference she was drawing from.

It was an older man, wrinkled around the eyes and mouth. The photo was taken from an album, she told me, of her entire family. Looking at his face, I thought I could see a slight resemblance; perhaps somewhere around the ears.

I asked her why she used the photo as a reference—couldn't she simply memorize his face?—and she laughed. "There are so many little things I'd never remember to put in without looking. The lid of his left eye comes up just a little bit more. And the right—there's a birthmark right here. He has a scar on the left side of his chin, and there are deeper wrinkles on this side of his mouth..."

She took a moment to look at the picture again. I had already memorized each of these details with my first viewing, and was at a slight loss for something to do. Tilting my head, I looked at it again. There was nothing new to notice; every mark was already imprinted on my mind—but the woman kept her face down and continued to study the photograph.

After a few moments, I left.

**

When I arrived on the third day, I was told that I smelled of the forest. I suppose I was aware of this, but it was still very strange to be randomly accosted by irrelevant facts. I told the woman to open a window, which she did—but not, she said, because she minded. Apparently she liked the smell of leaves.

I helped silently as she gathered paints, buckets, wipes, turpentine, and paper towels; and watched as she buzzed around the kitchen to see if there was anything she had forgotten. There was not, but I felt that telling her would not help anything. Instead, I decided to conquer the art of making tea.

When I returned, I found that she had already begun her work again. I watched as she leaned back, examined the painting as a whole, and then moved forward to paint the corner of an eye. She stood up to look at the image, squinting at its fuzzy details, and I assumed, correctly, that she had not managed to memorize it overnight.

"You could not possibly need this portrait," I said. The woman continued to paint, now measuring with her hands where on the canvas she wanted to mark out different features. This seemed useless.

"Don't you want to know my name?"

"I want to know why you are painting this portrait," I said, and paused. Something there felt incorrect. Yes—It was impolite to change the subject, and I had broken the rules. I decided to fix things with another human ritual. "Please."

(All better.)

"Yuna," she said, beginning to shade the left eye. After a moment, she paused and attempted to cover up the shading with new paint. It appeared she had made another mistake. "Yuna Hahn."

"You have photography. You couldn't possibly need a double. Are you planning to sell it?"

She turned, and I caught for the first time the possibility of frustration.

"Go draw something."

I had never drawn anything, but it appeared that she wanted me to be out of the way for the moment, so I brought her some more turpentine and went hunting for pen and paper.

Drawing was not as difficult as I had thought. I did wonder for a moment what the woman intended for me to draw, given that she had not specified, but I supposed it was not quite as important as the getting-out-of-the-way implication of the instruction.

So I drew her.

It came out perfectly, as expected; forever there would be a piece of the woman existing within the paper. For some reason.

It had not taken five minutes, so I made another drawing. I continued in this manner until I had used up several pieces of paper. There were painting women all over the table.

Around this point, the kettle came to a boil, and I poured the tea for her. She came shuffling into the kitchen in her pink slippers and tried to find a place to put her tea down before noticing what was preventing her from using the table.

"Oh!"

I looked in the kettle. There was too much tea left; I was not planning on drinking any and it would be very difficult to make it appear as though I had.

"You drew—a lot. Oh, my God—is this me?"

I was not certain as to why she was asking. Of course it was her; who else would it be? It was a perfect representation. While she was turned away, I poured some tea out into the sink. Perhaps I could hold up an empty cup and pretend I was drinking out of it.

"I love these." She picked up two and compared them, holding one in each hand. Then she put them down and picked up another piece. "Can I keep one?"

yves.

"You can keep all of them." I began stacking the drawings.

The woman made an interested noise and sat down to sip her tea. I investigated the progress on her painting.

She was now three days in, and it was still incomplete. There was only one visible eye, floating in a peach-dark sea of paint. The background seemed to simply be the white of the canvas.

"You're taking a long time," I said, and she looked up.

"I like to paint in my own way." She stood up to get sugar, and I considered the purple and red streaks throughout the piece. The black-and-white photo certainly did not appear to have such colorful skin.

"What do you mean?"

She looked surprised at my question, and took her tea with her to look at the painting. A dangerous exercise, given humanity's propensity towards randomly tripping and falling and spilling things, but perhaps understandable when one took into account the fact that humanity was infinitely careless as well.

"I don't want it to look *exactly* like the photo. I want to show how *I* see him." She traced, in the air, some planes of his face, bringing her smallest finger across the canvas to aid her great sweeps of explanation. Style, uniqueness, individual content. I listened carefully, and she asked if my question was answered.

"Yes."

(No.)

We stood together in silence for a moment, and then she stepped back to the table with her mostly-empty teacup. I watched her refill it before glancing back at the painting. It looked subtly different, somehow.

"I think you should try drawing like that," she said, gently picking up the top drawing from my stack. I looked at it with her, not understanding. "With your own style. Your drawings are beautiful, but they're also..."

I waited.

"They're photographic." She smiled. "I see why you think we only *need* photographs."

This was not an explanation that made any sense.

"Listen," she tried. "I think you should draw something stylized. A little different from reality. *Show* me the difference between drawings and photos."

"How?" I asked, and she handed me the pencil. Our eyes met.

The light was filtering through her hair. There was a brightness to her eyes that I had not noticed before. It came to me that, with her rough skin and chapped lips, there was a cast to her human features that I would never know.

"Don't make it quite so perfect," she said, smiling. "Show me how *you* draw. Be a bit original; make a few mistakes."

She looked at me, and I looked back at her. Then my gaze slipped down to the pencil in my hand, and I saw my fingers tighten around it.

"I can't."

strawberry syrup.

Her day is officially gelato university, ice cream shop job, night shift at the hospital, but unofficially she is also dealing blood on the side, and that's what suits her best. Lily likes to be busy.

Two scoops strawberry; one vanilla; two bananas, each halved and poked in where there's room. Then whipped cream, a cherry, and sprinkles only on the side. Lily does it all, and she does it fast, and after that she is off to the bathroom to take the call that has been buzzing in her phone all afternoon.

"I need—uh—how do you measure blood," says the voice on the other end. Lily is smooth, and she uses a fake English accent, because that's how you get the brand out.

"It's in liters, hon; just check the site."

"I need... Hold on." Clicking, clicking, clicking.

"We have half price on gallons," she says, gently. "Just in case. And you can keep it for a little while, too, if you don't finish it off in the first couple of days." She looks into the mirror, checking her lipstick.

"Okay." Long pause. *"Costs... two... three thousand?"*

"Yes; we have a Paypal." Pause again, wait for confirmation...

yves.

"Okay. Oh, I found it. Okay. Thanks."

"Welcome!" she chirps, and it's back to ice cream serving for her.

Milkshake; this one wants whipped cream on top and two straws; one for each girlfriend. Made with black cherry ice cream, which means all the little cherry bits grind about in the mixer as Lily makes it.

Vanilla, strawberry slices, whipped cream, cherry. Lily hands it over with a big smile, and the child involved gasps at how big the sundae is.

Her phone buzzes. Lily ignores it, tucking a strand of pink hair behind her ear. Hero? Not this early, certainly; she knows Lily's got her shift. Another order, this one for strawberry/lemon-lime, and they want a soda, too. It's always busy Lily's time of day; her hands fly and her phone buzzes. Again.

Milkshake with two scoops of strawberry and one of vanilla; whipped cream and cherry on top, hand off.

Her professor.

"You *do* work here!" Extra smiles. "Of course, of course, it's so cute... But is it *authentic?*"

She secretly strongly dislikes (not hates—Lily never hates) this

123

one. He's obsessed with *authenticity;* why can't she just serve cute ice cream? It just so happens that this shop is not at all authentic, which is supposed to be the *point,* so she tells him that and he orders one scoop of chocolate just to humor her.

Her pink streak is ruined.

Lily sighs and runs into the bathroom again; the texts are from her mother. *When are you visiting?* and *I need to know how many places to set for Thanksgiving.* It is still August. Lily sends back a harried *I hope I can make it but I don't know, Mom, sorry* and speeds back into the shop.

Fifteen minutes 'til closing. Time to put the sign out? No, but she does it anyway; she's had two orders waiting since this morning and if she doesn't get to the hospital in time tonight it's all blown. Mostly her mind is with the witch; whoever she is, the first thing she said to Lily was a mildly bemused *"That accent is fake,"* and it didn't get much better from there.

"Seven hundred? Are you serious? I could get—Listen, this is for—Work—Very important—"

"How can you possibly not have discounts, please, I can look into your future if you'd like—"

"Yes, it is very urgent; I'm sorry, I was only told today but I

yves.

need it, it's for this scrying bowl—"

"Good lord, that's absurd. I might as well have them ship it from back home at this rate..."

And then there had been a hurried deal regarding once-in-a-lifetime discounts and a thousand thank yous and Lily had had another full liter of blood on her plate. Which, coupled with the order from the vampire from before and the vampire from just now, was going to be impossible to find.

And then there's whoever-it-is stealing blood from the hospital and leaving rumpled twenties in their wake. That's definitely not helping, and if it happens tonight Lily will have three orders impossible to complete. If she were a less busy person, of course, she'd investigate, but there's already someone named Odde on the case *and* it's time to start mopping. Lily grabs the dirty thing from the supply closet and begins dragging it across the floor in the back; her sullen coworker, having already put the sign out, starts coming around to people's tables to make them mildly uncomfortable and slightly more ready to go home.

Lily has a home to go to, for that matter—Hero. But Hero is used to late returns, and so far there haven't been any urgent texts—Lily still remembers the day of *the pipe just broke so I'm calling a plumber / the plumber seems to be making it worse /*

computing a potential solution / the plumber did not appreciate my numerical advice / the plumber is angry; the pipe is fixed / how are things?.

She takes a taxi home, using the extra time to shoot off texts to as many people as possible: *coming back now* to Hero (she receives a heart emoji in return, which makes her own heart jump), *There's been a bit of a hold up due to a large volume of orders; most likely we'll be able to get you your blood by tomorrow, though!* to the witch, vampire, and vampire #2, and a long-winded apology to her mom for not being around often enough.

There, she thinks, that ought to hold them for a while.

By the time she gets home, she has six more texts.

Hero opens the door to find Lily looking at her phone, which is one of the many things that makes Hero frown (others include concentration, difficult physical tasks, and dogs). Lily holds up a finger—*I'm sorry, but I have two other orders, and supply is very difficult to find, as I'm sure you know* has to be sent out to vampire #1, who has just sent her *I think you don't realize that if I don't get this tonight I am going to die.*

Then she looks up, grins only slightly nervously, and gives Hero a full-body hug, which makes Hero smile at least a little bit.

yves.

They are an odd set of roommates; so far, only Lily's mother has commented, because nobody else has noticed (they live slightly off-campus, and Hero is a hermit.) Lily has already found an apartment by her second year of college because she is 1) very savvy, 2) very sweet, and 3) slightly rich. Or she *was,* before the rent hit.

Lily is very lucky. She is pink-haired, blue-eyed, and the precise sort of bouncy, pastel-wearing kind of girl (woman? she can't believe she's nineteen) who puts everyone at ease, which means stealing and dealing blood is a snap. Hero (pre-name and gender marker change: Hiro), on the other hand, is dark-haired, dark-eyed, and a very specific type of pretty that appears engineered to seduce women... unless that's just Lily. From there things run in a rather similar pattern: Hero lives in her computer, Lily lives for pen and paper; Hero keeps her hair about an inch long, Lily can put hers up in a bun with strands left over; Hero can't cook, Lily—is already running to the stove with distinct fear on her face.

"Sorry," Hero says, hands already in her pockets, and Lily makes a few choked noises (there is only-slightly-dissipated smoke in the air) before slamming open a drawer and grabbing a spatula.

"Hero," she says, and Hero comes in to lean casually on the

doorframe. She is apparently unaware of what Loosely Sexual Lounging does to Lily. (In essence: makes it suddenly impossible to find the spatula.)

Lily's phone is already buzzing with several new texts, and then it begins the persistent vibration pattern of a call. She slams the found spatula onto the stove after one crack at whatever is crusting burntly over one of the spirals, then yanks Hero over to get rid of the rest.

"Should I be worried?" says the voice at the other end, and it is British and already worried so Lily doesn't really know what to do with it. She makes her voice British, too.

"Not necessarily *worried,* no, but I understand your order was urgent and so I wanted to warn you that you might... need to consider an alternate plan just in case," she says, turning to monitor Hero's progress on the stove (bad). Hero has some sharp ears; Lily is going to have to be creative about this. "Look, I'll call you back as soon as I see what the situation is; I really hope I'll be able to get you what you need."

Sigh from the other end.

"I hope so, too," says the British witch, and the line clicks off.

Lily buries her face in her hands.

"Etsy orders?" Hero asks, sounding very perceptive from her position by the horrifically mangled stove.

"They don't have enough clay at the store," Lily says, "and just get that thing off before dinner, alright?"

She has no idea why Hero decided to cook dinner tonight; this is literally *the worst night* possible for her to have decided to cook dinner; *why is she doing this.*

Lily pulls three boxes of microwavable soup out of the pantry and starts microwaving them all together; the call from the hospital has to be held to her ear.

"Are you available tonight?"

"Um, yes, yes, definitely, I'll just be—I think I might be a bit late, I—" nervous laugh—"my friend burned dinner, so I'll have to—"

"Detective Odde is looking to talk to all of the nurses. If you're on shift tonight, you have to find her by my desk afterwards."

"Thanks," Lily says, feeling miserable. She took this job because she knew she wouldn't need much sleep, but after-hours interviews were not part of that calculation, and things are suddenly looking Bad.

Her soup-dinner is a mild failure (Hero loathes cream-ofpotato, which is naturally all they have left), but Lily feels better afterwards. She changes out of the shop uniform and into the white nurse one, showering in between, and is even brave enough to give a surprised Hero another hug before she goes out.

"Etsy again?" Hero drawls, and Lily rolls her eyes.

"You *know* I work at the hospital some nights," she says, flipping her hair out of her collar. Hero shrugs and turns back to whatever freelance coding she's been assigned this week, and Lily runs out the door to get her taxi.

Gelato school is not as interesting as it sounds. Lily is thinking about it tonight because she has been tossing around the idea of dropping out; it looked nice with her cute ice cream server persona, but now it's just getting in the way. If she wasn't sitting through *How Gelato Got Its Name* lectures and *Make Your Own Chocolate!* seminars, she might be out in taxis taking her to other hospitals, where she could expand her illicit dealings.

And it seems a little silly, at times, to work with the school when she could be spending more time at the shop. Her boss has been hinting and hinting at full-time openings, but it's not like Lily has the time right now, even if she does love it more than anything else in the world. Except possibly Hero and ice cream itself.

This is what Lily is thinking about when she arrives.

Lily hops out and runs in; she has become adept at modifying her own files. *Hero* has, really, but Lily borrows the technique and uses it to delete tasks she's been given, bend her hours, and generally make it look like she's a much more productive member of the hospital than she really is.

Other things she does: put in a whole lot of extra demands for blood to be sent to certain rooms. Tonight, having done just that, she takes the blood bag off the tray the second it's wheeled into the room; both patients are asleep and won't notice a thing. She repeats this process, using a combination of fake names and a blonde wig she's keeping in her bag, until all that's left is to just steal a couple of extra bags and then she *still* does not have enough and she is two hours off of her shift being over and her phone is buzzing again.

Do you have it now?

Sorry but I really need it

And from the other vampire:

Hey do you have the blood —I'm really hurting

She texts both of them something related to her doing her best and takes a deep breath. It's fine. This is fine. She can't take any more without actually causing a shortage, but—there are other ways.

SOMETHING'S NOT RIGHT

Lily knows where the supplies are kept. She pulls them into a supply closet, along with a chair and her things. When she shuts the door, the only light comes from a bulb that hangs from the ceiling. She takes a deep breath and sticks the needle in her arm.

This is her secret: She is painfully, horribly averse to real blood. Real, actual blood coming out of someone's body, that is; not the bags at her feet. Looking at her arm makes her head spin. She turns away and thinks about ice cream. She is only an ice cream server, only a Gelato Academy student, only a girl with pink hair, only, only...

One scoop strawberry, one scoop vanilla, hot fudge on top.

Two scoops black cherry, whipped cream, maraschino cherry on top.

One scoop vanilla, sprinkles.

Gelato is an art, a tradition; if you are in this class today, you are willing to embrace and continue that tradition. Gelato must be hand-crafted, natural, milky...

Three scoops black cherry, hot fudge, sprinkles.

One cup milk, stir... Are you listening? Hey, Lily, wake up. Milk?

Lily? Lily. Lily. Lily. Lily—

"Oh..." Lily's head hurts. Is that Hero?

"Lily, you have to tell them—"

"Hm?" She's so sleepy... Is she in bed? No, the bed's moving... Her hair is all out of place; she wants to ask Hero to fix it...

"Lily, are you human?" Hero squeezes her hand; shakes it. Her face is white and shimmering in Lily's vision. "Lily, you have to tell them."

Why would Hero ask that? Lily closes her eyes.

"Lily—" Hero says, and her voice breaks. "Tell me, are you human?"

Lily opens her mouth. She's so tired...

"Yes," she whispers, and falls asleep.

When she wakes up next, she is a little more aware of her surroundings. She's in a hospital bed. It is warm. Hero is sitting in her chair, fiddling with her—

"My phone!"

Hero looks up. The phone is half-apart in her hands. This is something she does when she is stressed; but—

"Lily," she says, and snaps everything together; she leans right across the bed and squeezes Lily; hard.

"Ow," Lily squeaks.

"I followed you," Hero says. She grins. "Sorry."

"You... followed...?"

"I thought you were involved in drugs," Hero says, looking a little bit pink around the cheeks. Lily laughs.

"No, no, it was only... the blood!" She sits straight up, and her head spins. She flops over again; "oooh..."

"Don't worry; I got it to everyone," Hero says. Lily squints at her. "Your password is *PINK*, I got it on the first try."

Lily can't parse any of this, but the mention of her phone makes her remember something else.

"British witch..." she mumbles.

"British—oh! The girl with the ponytail. She came in after I gave her a call and... well, she was a little bit terrified, and she handed me some kind of bottle and told me to make you drink it. Which I did, and then you woke up, so I suppose it... did some good... She was muttering something about freelance witchcraft and pottery—Do you feel weird?"

"Not... any weirder than I should... blood," Lily says, closing her eyes. "That was stupid."

"It *was,*" Hero says, squeezing Lily's hand. "Look, I know you wanted to help people... But you're taking a break now. At least while you're living with me."

"Mhm." Mostly, Lily is happy to lie here and have Hero fuss over her. *Hero is better at this than cooking,* she thinks, somewhat out of tune.

"The, ah, odd woman," says Hero, and Lily blinks a couple times. *The what?* "The Odde woman." *Oh.* "She wants to talk to you. Fortunately..."

"Mm?"

"I told her you're my girlfriend and I know you better than that," Hero says, removing one hand from Lily's grasp to push her glasses up on her nose. Her cheeks pinken slightly.

Girlfriend?! shrieks the most coherent part of Lily's brain, completely ecstatically.

"Mm-hm," is all she manages, but Hero grins so charmingly that Lily suddenly has the power to see into the future, just like the British witch: a tri-scoop lemon sundae with strawberry syrup, whipped cream, a gummy bow, a maraschino cherry, and little pink candy beads for Lily, something less pink for Hero—maybe minty apple or chocolate with whipped cream and some matcha; Lily thinks Hero would like that. Lily's been saving those retired sugar Hello Kitty toppers for weeks now; maybe those on top...

"Hero..." she tries, and Hero leans in to listen. "...Go out with me..."

"Okay," Hero says, so soft, slipping her hand back into Lily's. And with that resolved, Lily finds herself falling asleep, and beginning to dream of angry professors shouting at her for putting blood in the gelato... *You disrespect the tradition! You thin the gelato with your bodily fluids! You are forever expelled from the Gelato Academy!...*

six hours under.

The woman on the L train is crying. Their shoulders are shaking, their knees are shaking, and their hands are up around their eyes, doing very little to quell the flow. Lons looks at them and feels a little bit wrong about herself—because she has a job to get to, and she has a presentation to give, and she has a desperate hatred for getting-involved-in-things, but now all of those 'has's are starting to seem a lot more like 'had's, because nobody *else* is getting involved, and the woman on the L train is crying.

Lons has probably been staring at the woman for a little too long, because all of a sudden they look up and Lons meets their eyes and they have these really nice, soft, earthy-brown eyes that twinkle a little, and Lons gets the feeling they'd be twinkling in a smile, too, and of course the woman gets up and reseats themself to the spot right next to Lons.

Well: the spot was empty, and Lons *did* tap it. Just a bit.

"I like your pin," Lons says, and the woman looks down at the ten separate pins littering the left side of their shirt. Grumpy Cat pins, lesbian flag pins, pins with little bits of text like "*HIGH FEMME PRINCESS*" or "*THEY/THEM, PLEASE*". There's a little pin with a mini-Death Star on it that says "*ceci n'est pas une lune*", but Lons doesn't understand that one beyond the artistic reference and direct French translation.

The woman smiles. This, of course, was the intended goal of the compliment, but now Lons suddenly realizes she has never wanted anything more than to help this woman on the L train. In fact, she desperately *needs* to get involved.

Ah, the perils of loving women.

Because Lons asks for the woman's name, and they say it's Flos ("Flows?" "Flos." "Floss?" "Flos." "Floes?" "Don't worry about it,") and Lons asks how their day is going, and they say it's fine ("Really?" "No,") and Lons asks what's wrong and they say "I'm dead."

Which is genuinely difficult for Lons to address, given that this can either be hyperbole or insanity, and either way it doesn't generally sound like the tone Lons wants anyone she knows to speak in.

"I'm sorry," she says, which is what she has learned to do when someone comes to her with an unrelatable problem.

"No, I—I mean it," says the woman, and they wave their hands a little and give off a general feeling of being about to burst into tears again, so Lons reaches over and gives them a comforting pat on the back and then leans back into her own personal space. The woman holds out a hand, pauses, collects themself to a reasonable degree, and continues. "I have—this quest, and it's impossible, and I'm going to die, and I don't—want to—"

"Neither do I, generally," Lons says, hoping this will keep the woman pacified, but it doesn't, and they collapse into Lons' lap.

"*NOW ARRIVING AT TOWNSEND STATION*," says a tinny voice over the train's speakers, and Flos instantly leaps up, which almost sends their head into a fatal collision with Lons'.

"That's my stop," they say, and look up at Lons.

Lons has a job. Lons has a presentation. Lons has, Lons has, Lons has a lot of feelings about this woman who may or may not be dying and sometimes Lons *has* heard of witches or werewolves or the sort of demons who live off Post Street, and the Medieval Literature and Conspiracy Fairy Tales class she took in college did have some grains of truth to it, so, under pressure, Lons takes a very large leap of faith.

"I'll help you," she says, and Flos brightens, which does a lot for them looks-wise—not that they needed it.

Lons sighs, and knows this will go badly.

**

Fifteen minutes and a few steps out into the street later, Lons is regretful. Already. Coincidentally, she is also on the phone with the employer she was supposed to be preparing to give a presentation to.

"I understand," she says, and then, looking over at Flos, "Family emergency. Couldn't be helped. I apologize. Yes, sir. Yes. I'm very sorry, sir."

"Sorry," Flos squeaks, in a sort of high-pitched echo, but Lons shakes her head and replaces her phone in her briefcase. It's superbly odd; carrying a briefcase around while wearing a dress that looks like it was made by someone in the midst of a torrid love affair with the fifties. Unfortunately, she was told she had to start dressing 'more femininely,' and she did already have the white heels in the back of her closet, so here she is, dressed very well for a meeting and very poorly for saving someone's life. "I think we need to take a cab—from here—"

Flos looks sort of uncertainly out at the street.

"Yes," Lons says, and Flos sighs and steps out into the street.

The directions Flos gives are vague and half-remembered, and Lons is forced to use some of her own knowledge of the city to translate them into genuine locations for their driver. She thinks, mostly, that they are headed towards the dock, so she offers that.

The silence that covers them is deeply uncomfortable.

"So am I allowed to look at you, or will all be lost?" Lons asks eventually. Flos looks up at her, seemingly not comprehending. "Because I think it might be too late for that."

Flos' fingers, decked out in slightly-chipped red nail polish, twitch uncertainly.

"What?"

Lons sighs deeply.

"Orpheus," she says. "And Eurydice."

And when Flos doesn't seem any more aware of the reference, Lons decides to just drop it; at the very least, Lons doesn't think looking at Flos will actually do anything, because that would imply that Lons would need to lead them out of the Underworld, and if that was the subway, then firstly, apt metaphor, and secondly, Flos would have disappeared back into it by now. So it looks like she's going to have to find another method of solving this.

"You're dying?" she asks, just to be entirely sure. Flos nods.

"I'm dying."

"You're dying."

"Yes."

"How?"

And Flos waves their hands, and shrugs, and looks out the window, and then begins.

Flos' story, as it happens, begins with their death. It begins with their death and goes from there, to being in a strange place, and being regretful and crying, and then miraculously being offered the choice of a quest. A quest involving reaching the location of their death by midday, which will apparently bring them back to life.

"Is that all?" Lons asks, somewhat wary. Flos cocks their head, and they do admit that it seems a little plain for a life-saving quest, but that's really all they were told. After all, if hints were given to everyone who asked for a second chance, the world would dissolve into chaos.

There are *rules* to this sort of thing.

**

Lons and Flos have to walk to the ferry service, because the location Lons asked the taxi to drop them off at was actually several blocks down from where they were supposed to end up, and this means that Lons is forced to clomp down the sidewalk in her white high heels. Flos is wearing heels, too, actually; red ones; and they handle their feet a lot better. Also, the heels go nicely with their fishnets, which they are (unfortunately) wearing under a pair of jean shorts.

Halfway down the first block, Lons takes off her shoes and holds them in her hands.

They find their way to the proper ferry service, somehow, and Lons hastily shoves her high heels back on as Flos asks how much it'll be and offers several handfuls of change. Lons comes up with the rest, somehow, and the two of them board the ferry with all the others interested in early-morning ferry rides—which is to say, almost no one.

The ride is extremely long, and Flos is impatient; rubbing their heels together and jumping around on the upper deck. Lons considers taking off her jacket and giving it to Flos, but that would only make *her* cold. She's also not sure if it would even fit Flos, given that Lons is small and sticklike and occasionally considers shopping in the children's section, while Flos is chubby and soft and rather deceptively tall, even without the heels.

Flos' breath shines in the air, and Lons stands a little nearer so as to warm them.

"What happens, hypothetically," she asks, "if I don't save you?"

SOMETHING'S NOT RIGHT

"Then I die," Flos says, very matter-of-factly, and Lons sighs and hands them the jacket. Flos happily slides it over their shoulders, covering whatever it is that gets covered, and looks up to the sky. The sun rises slowly higher. With Lons' watch reading a very unsteady nine o'clock sort of time, it'll be nine thirty when the ferry arrives. Lons steps closer to Flos and uses their height to, very inconspicuously, lean on them.

**

Once on land, Flos is back to sprinting. Lons sees that they've removed their party heels (Lons' own shoes are long gone) to more easily run across the broken sidewalk of the island. Lons hurries after them, looking ahead and behind to watch for cars on the lonely road. None follow.

Their destination is a small, shaded, heavily sandy alcove beneath the bridge connecting the island to the city across from it. Flos veers off the road and heads straight for the bridge, where they run down the hill (still in fishnets, though heavily torn by now) and collapse on the sand. Lons comes after, slightly more gracefully, and follows Flos' gaze under the bridge.

There's a body.

A greying, silent body.

yves.

The skull is fractured; blood and grey matter is floating softly on the water. The limbs are splayed. One hand is disturbed only slightly by the waves, which pull gently at it on the shore. The entire corpse is half-in, half-out of the water.

Lons runs.

She runs through the sand and the water and the rocks in her wide-ripped tights and drops to the ground before the body. She has a high tolerance for blood, that's alright, she took several classes on proper medical procedures and had to look at a lot of detailed illustrations—but it's *dead.* This is, *was,* a person, and is not anymore. Lons looks up, to where the body fell—jumped—came from. The bridge.

Her breath comes sharply in her throat.

"I didn't think it was real," Flos whispers.

Lons looks up, one hand before the body's. Several strands of her long hair are leaning across her face.

"I thought maybe—it was all a dream." Flos blinks several times, and continues staring at the body. Their fishnets are torn all up one side.

Fishnets—

Lons looks at the body before her.

Fishnets.

White shirt. Jean shorts. Red nail polish. Dark, dark hair, which swirls and floats across the thin sheen of water now covering half of the dead Flos' downturned face.

Lons propels herself backwards, scrabbling against the dirt and sand for purchase. The dead Flos—the not-Flos—lies half in the water, unchanged, and the water continues its soft embrace. Back and forth, back and forth the shallow water flows.

This is a *recent* death.

Of course, it must have been—last night—

But no. The body is pale, but still almost-warm. It's kept its shape. The shirt—the shirt is white, clean, simply clinging wetly to Flos' side. The *dead* Flos' side.

It's as if they'd only just—

"I'm sorry," Flos whispers. "I didn't think—"

"I didn't think, either," Lons says, and laughs in a hollow, quiet sort of way. "Oh, God."

"It was an accident," Flos says, and Lons props herself against the leg of the bridge. She's hunched over, wet, and being dripped on by the underside of it, but she'll take anything if it means not being near—that. Flos. Flos' death.

"It does not," Lons manages, "look like an accident."

Flos nods, and takes a deep, shuddering breath, and Lons puts a hand to her head, because this is all so terribly, incredibly wrong. She didn't ask for this. She woke up this morning to go to her job. This is all wrong; someone else should be here.

"I don't know what to do."

Lons turns, very slowly, towards Flos. Flos is facing her, earnest, small strands of hair blowing into their eyes. They are so physical, and so alive, and this morning Lons thought they were pretty.

This morning Lons still, desperately, in some way disconnected from reality, thinks they are pretty.

Standing, careful of the low rise of the bridge, Lons looks down at her legs. Her legs, not the body. She is not shaking.

Flos watches as Lons steps over to them; purposefully, strongly. She clenches her fists, and her nails bite into the palms of her hands. She thinks of Flos' dead hands, being slowly embalmed by water.

There is nothing Flos can do. These are the end of the instructions; and Flos is going to die here.

Lons sits down, back to the corpse, and looks at Flos. She

realizes now, that Flos is wearing lip gloss. A thin peach-pink façade of glitter on their lips. It makes them look even softer, and Lons' breath catches painfully.

So she kisses them.

Flos is warm, and soft, and Lons can feel their skin and muscle and bone as much as she can any other woman; they're solid and real and they put one hand up to hold her head closer to theirs, and when they pull away she can see the flush on their face.

They are so alive.

The sun is hovering somewhere above their backs. Flos looks out across the ocean pensively, and Lons thinks for a moment on anything else she can say, another way to distract from the moment. There is one more hour for Flos to exist.

"It was worth it," Flos says quietly, and Lons looks at them. They take a breath and look out across the water, then catch Lons' eyes again. "To—do all this. Even if we failed."

"Yes," Lons says, though she doesn't believe it. Inside, she is a roiling mess of storm clouds and angry fear, and she desperately wants to change something, but she doesn't know how or what to do.

Being here didn't work. Kissing Flos didn't work; and some

part of Lons thought that it would—Snow White style. Not that she wouldn't have done it otherwise...

And then Lons' fingers pull together in the sand, curling into fists again, and she is on the *verge* of an idea, but it is insane and ridiculous and she may be sitting on the beach at eleven fifteen in the morning with no shoes and an arm-length rip in her tights, but she can't—she doesn't—

When Lons looks over at Flos again, they're back to crying, and a single strand of their hair is fluttering in the wind.

Lons scrambles over to the corpse. It's almost-floating in the water, still, right under the bridge, and she turns it over *(don't think about it don't think about it)* and looks into its eyes, and it is a smooth porcelain doll version of Flos. Pale, cold, glassy and glittery over the lips. It is impossible for there to be glitter on the lips, and yet.

"Don't talk me out of this," Lons says, and half-laughs. Perhaps she is delirious. "I know my fairy tales."

Flos looks over at her.

"Don't talk me out of it, I said," Lons says, and bends. Her breath ghosts over the corpse's lips, and her voice is suddenly only a whisper. "Oh, God."

She kisses the corpse.

What she tells herself is, interestingly, not that she is kissing Flos—she tells herself that she is kissing a statue, because statues are just as dull and lifeless and they are very cold and stiff and once-upon-a-time in an art museum downtown Lons saw two girls wait for the docents to turn away before they kissed one of the Rodins, and Lons was jealous.

Then the corpse *moves,* and Lons makes a desperate attempt to fling it away from herself and swim backwards, Flos be damned, life be damned, ocean be damned she is not getting involved with the *undead* (though, of course, it is a little too late to think that) and then Flos sits up out of the water.

"Oh, hells," Lons says, and she's barely breathing. Her face is wet.

Flos coughs several times, flipping their wet hair out of their eyes. Their skin is clean and slick; as rosy as the live Flos'—but when Lons looks over to where Flos was just sitting, they're gone, without even the slightest trace. Lons crouches, shakily, and begins to crawl past the suddenly-revived Flos when they turn to look at her for the first time.

"Oh," they say, and their eyes are very wide and new. Lons gets to her feet and looks down at them, breathing hard. "Do I know you?"

Lons looks at them. Their fishnets are ripped, slightly, just at the knee and sole of one foot, and if she had just met them, she would have assumed it was purposeful. Their red nail polish is clearly self-done; bits and pieces are half-overflowing onto the skin of their fingers.

It would be so easy; so, *so* easy to lie. She can go back—today, she can go back to her job. She's never missed a day before; her life can be the same as it always was. She doesn't have to bother with this any longer.

Flos' hands are wet, and soft, and the tips of their fingertips are slightly blue.

Lons tells the truth.

monsters and The Guy.

It's not so strange to see monsters in the boarding line. Men with lobster claws or women with the heads of birds. Sometimes a siren needs to fly, too, and if the blood dripping off her claws gets onto your suitcase, well, that's just your fault for not flying first class. She has to sign six different forms to ensure that she won't crash the plane, you have to get a little blood on your things. Suck it up and drive next time, you know?

You know.

Anyway, that's normal. What isn't normal is The Guy.

I wouldn't have noticed The Guy if I hadn't lost gate A7. It happens all the time, really—you get to the airport, you get your ticket, you realize your gate is somewhere else. You know, not... past the GATES A1-10 sign. And the place where A7 is supposed to be is just, you know, an empty room with a bunch of classroom desks in it. It sucks, but there it is. Or isn't.

So I had to find the front desk—which wasn't missing, thank *God*—and I got to talk to this pretty witch with a little name tag that had a bunch of ampersands and a hydra on it, and she was kind enough to tell me that gate A7 was hiding out with the G gates today. So that was nice. And, you know, I was just about to head off when the three-eyed guy with peach-colored hair behind her said, "The Guy's back in Arrivals. Should we send someone down?" and she sort of looked at me like he wasn't supposed to say things like that in front of, you know, passengers, or maybe humans, so I got the hell out of there but before I did I definitely saw her nod.

So. A Guy. The Guy. Back in Arrivals.

I wondered the whole way down to the gate about him, and also the whole way down to my seat, and then... pretty much until I got off the plane. And I guess I would've forgotten about him, but then I came back, and now I'm here in Arrivals and there is definitely a guy. The Guy, I suppose.

He's dark-haired, sort of, and I say 'sort of' because he has waist-length straight hair that probably used to be brown (brown eyebrows... always a solid giveaway) but has been dyed mostly black with some red and white streaks. He's human—I think. And he's wearing a suit, which goes great with the hair. Tanned skin. Sharp nose. Very sad-looking.

That's how I know it's him. I was wondering if maybe I wouldn't know, or if he'd be just any other guy and I'd miss him, but he's different from everyone else.

I guess I didn't know until now that there was a look for this— a look for someone who shouldn't be waiting anymore. Everyone around him is holding signs or bags or something, and they all have this completely different look; this wide, alert look, because they know whoever they're waiting for will be there in a minute.

The Guy doesn't look like that. He looks like someone who's been waiting for a long, long time, who's already sort of given up on waiting.

He also looks like a guy who could use some company.

So I walk up to him.

"Hey," I say. He looks me up and down and breathes this little sigh of relief before turning back to look into the crowd.

"You're not one of them," he says. "Okay."

It's kind of hard to respond to that—especially when I don't know who 'they' are, or where to go from 'okay.'

"Them?" I ask, because that's a start, and he shrugs.

"Airport workers. They usually come later, anyway. Tell me to get out. Creeps them out that I stand here every day, apparently."

I try not to mention that it is, you know, kind of creepy when you just stand in the same place every day. I mean, maybe if he was doing something... but it doesn't look like he is. He's just, well, standing.

"You don't take a break ever?" I ask. He shrugs again. It's a very weird look in a suit.

"I have to go to the bathroom," he says. "I'm not a—" and then he says something that I'm sure is some type of obscure monster, but I can't make out how it's pronounced or written. "And sometimes I eat."

He glances over to the Cinnabon nearest us, and that reassures me somewhat. No really frightening person can eat at Cinnabon.

"But otherwise, you just stand here," I say, and he nods. I'd ask about jobs and hobbies and such, but some people really don't have those. At this point, I've learned not to bother.

So instead, I look for the nearest seat and take it.

He turns to look at me, surprised.

"I'm waiting with you," I say. "Got nowhere to be. Still looking for work, you know."

He nods, though I'm not sure if he does know, and turns back to his waiting.

You know, funny thing about watching someone just stand in the middle of a room: it's really, *really* boring.

I dig out my computer and start combing through job search sites, more to pass the time than anything else. It's hard to find work as a film major. I can edit, which is pretty good, but it still looks like nobody really needs my skills, and that sucks. I browse through a couple ads for wedding photographers before quitting and looking back up at The Guy.

"Who're you waiting for, again?" I ask, and he frowns before walking backwards towards me. That's a really, *really* weird look in a suit, and it also seems kind of useless, mostly because he's already turned around to look at me, so what does it matter where his body is facing when he walks, you know?

"I'm not sure," he says, sitting down and rearranging his suit jacket. A couple of women with lion's heads walk by us and glance at him oddly.

"You're not sure," I repeat. Because he's apparently been waiting long enough to establish a Cinnabon routine, but not long enough to figure out what exactly he's waiting for. And a couple thousand people walk through here each day, so it's pretty likely that he's already missed whoever it is.

"I saw them," he says, like he's explaining this to his sixth airport worker, "in a dream. It was very, very clear about the fact that I would meet them in an airport. In *this* airport. And so I gave up my life of video game development—"

"Your life of *what*—"

"—to meet my destiny. Do you have a dollar?" He holds out his hand.

I do have a dollar, but I don't have a job. And *he* apparently has the money for a really nice suit.

I give him the dollar anyway, and he returns in a moment with two cinnamon twists and two bottles of water.

"I was short thirty cents," he says, by way of explanation, and starts crunching away at his cinnamon twist in silence. I put a napkin in his lap, because that really is a fantastic suit. This is kind of painful to watch.

"Don't you think you'll run out of money at some point?" I manage between bites of cinnamon twist.

"Possibly," he says, and chews thoughtfully. "Maybe my fated person will have money to lend."

And he smiles in a way that doesn't go with the suit. Or the destiny.

So, of course, I tell him I'll see him tomorrow.

**

He's still there the next day. In the same spot, too. This time I bring him a sandwich, and sit down hopefully on those uncomfortable airport-seats. Halfway through my search for a charging port, he walks over and hands me the charger to his iPhone.

Wow.

I don't have an iPhone, and I'm trying to charge my computer.

I tell him that, and he shrugs and sits down next to me, re-training his eyes on the people walking around with their bags.

"You should get a Mac," he says, while eating his sandwich.

"You should get a napkin," I say, balancing between pulling out my computer and pointing to the pile of crumbs in his lap. He looks at them sort of boredly and brushes them away, which isn't really a solution to the problem. My computer whirrs.

He stares at my computer as it boots up, and I'm sure he's counting the seconds. It's not that slow—not for a three-year-old machine. And it runs The Sims just fine; so there.

Today's prospects aren't any better. There are people who want photos of their baby and people who want edits on their porn shoot, but I'm not interested in either of those things/people/situations, so I keep looking. If I had a degree, I could probably teach film somewhere. But, you know, I don't have a degree.

"The only thing PCs are good for is gaming," The Guy says, with his mouth almost entirely full of sandwich. I don't argue with him, mostly because I don't care.

There's some kind of TV show looking for editors. Apparently it's something I can do from home, which is nice, because I'm sort of bound to college right now. Unfortunately, the show's one of those pseudo-reality sitcom things, and I don't know how much I care about that. There are three episodes online, and I pull one of them up while The Guy watches.

"This is garbage," he says after a few minutes. "You really watch this?"

"Don't you have a person to wait for?" I ask, because he doesn't even have the audio for context, and he whips his head back up to look at the crowds of people swarming around the lobby. I pause the episode I'm watching and consider. It *is* garbage, unfortunately. But I could get used to it. I think.

I start drafting an email to the people who've posted the ad, pretending not to notice when The Guy glances over at it, which he does a lot. He makes it kind of difficult to type—e-mails are bad enough without someone staring over your shoulder. Still, I manage something, and he glances down at my email signature as I hit Send.

"Eliza Feldman," he reads. I nod. "Hey, I'm Jewish, too."

Small world.

"You have a name?" I ask, and he winces.

"Just call me Red."

"That bad, huh?"

"British *and* Israeli parents."

"Ouch."

Red, who I'm still sort of calling The Guy internally, watches as I look through a couple more offers. There are a lot of really bad wages attached to already-mediocre jobs, and Red insists on volunteering his opinions.

"That is *not* worth it," he says at some point, and I shut my computer as loud as I can. He jumps, which kind of makes me feel better.

"How are you going to know when you find who you're waiting for?" I ask, because I really can't stand to think about work for one more second. He shrugs, which is sort of enough of an answer.

"That was not explained to me," he says, and I remember how much I *really* hate oracles.

**

Looking for work kind of sucks no matter where you do it,

which is why I'm half-thinking of quitting my Red-watching gig at the airport. It doesn't actually promise anything more than the vague possibility of seeing whatever messianic figure Red is waiting for, and even that isn't likely. Also, he's still offering opinions on my computer.

I switch from Craigslist to video games, which makes me feel a lot better.

"What are you doing?" Red asks. He's magically appeared by my side again, in much the same way he has over the last week. It looks like I don't need to invite him over anymore, which is pretty good. At least it means I don't have to lure him with food.

"I'm taking a break," I say, which is true, except the break is going to be several hours long and I'm not going to do anything but play this one unbeatable game. Red watches for a while, occasionally glancing up to see if his person's showed yet. I still don't know exactly what he's looking for, and ask.

"I have no idea," he says, which is at least honest. My avatar catches another tiny ball of light. "The dream commanded me to *wait.* It did not say what I was supposed to wait for."

"What?" I ask, tapping a different key. "So it might not even be a person?"

"I'm sure it's a person," he says, very frustratedly, even though that doesn't seem clear at all to me. He could be waiting for the manager of Cinnabon, for all he knows. Speaking of which—I close my computer and hand him a couple dollars.

"Go get me a scone or something."

"They don't *have* scones," he says, but in a few minutes he's back with a really dumb-looking drink. I'm talking chocolate-syrup-over-whipped cream dumb. I mean, this thing has a tiny doughnut hole on top of it. When I say dumb, I mean dumb. And it's dumb.

"That is too much whipped cream," I tell him.

"You can handle it," he tells me.

"I'm lactose intolerant," I tell him.

He groans and angrily whips out a straw, which has got to be the *absolute* weirdest thing I've seen him do in that suit. Or a different suit; I'm not clear on whether he's washing it every night or just wearing identical ones. Anyway, he handles the whipped cream just fine.

"You owe me some food," I remind him, and when he stomps off to dispose of the drink he returns with a regular cinnamon bun. Thank God.

"Any details I can get out of you on this dream-prophecy?" I ask, and he frowns at me. "Because, just for the record, I'm a huge skeptic. And I hate oracles."

"I'm *not* an oracle," says The (Oracle) Guy, oracley, in response to being tagged as an oracle.

"Sure," I say, biting into the cinnamon bun. "And I'm not a filmmaker."

"You're not an *anything* without a job," he says, and I can see the smile's just there to make sure I'm not hurt. "*Especially* not while you're playing video games."

"I don't know," I say, and I punctuate the sentiment by leaning as far back as possible in my uncomfortable airport seat. "Seemed to work for you."

"I know *code,*" he says, as if that makes all the difference. "And design. I could build this entire world, if I wanted to." And he does this proud little hair-flip, which for a second makes him look kind of different—beyond *weird* in the suit, just sad. And wrong. Which is kind of a lot to get out of a hair flip, so I just sit there and stare at him for a moment.

"What?"

"Nothing," I say, looking down at the computer. "Except I

think you're wasting your life hanging out here. And you're not going to find anyone."

He doesn't say anything. When I look at him, he's already turned away, and there's a small pain in my chest over the look on his face. I go back to staring at my computer screen, and when I look up the next time, he's gone.

**

I guess he just needed a minute, because when I walk in the next day, Red confronts me almost instantly.

"It was a normal dream," he says. "At first. I don't remember what I was dreaming about, just that it was normal. And then it faded out and everything went white and it faded into this airport. Right here. And I saw myself standing here, in a suit, and someone walked up to me. I don't know who. I didn't see them. And then I kept having that dream, over and over, until I came here. Now it's stopped. Eliza, I know this is my destiny."

There's a long pause where I try to think of a witty comeback.

"Hello to you, too," I manage, which *sucks,* and I can tell that he knows that I know that it sucks, but he just sideways-grins and follows me over to the usual seat. I'm guessing this means I've been forgiven. It's fast, though I'm obviously not complaining.

"I shouldn't say it," he says as we sit down, "but I admit I'm close to giving up."

"Oh?" I don't really have anything specific to say to that. I guess that it's sad. And that it's unlike him. But I'm not going to say that, because 1) feelings aren't cool, and 2) I've barely known him a week.

"Yes." He glances over at a group of centaurs who are chattering away in a corner. One of them puts her phone to her ear and covers it with her hand, leaning in to listen. "Would you like a scone?"

I would, actually. So I let him go and get one, and I lean back on the weird black airplane seats to think.

There are thousands of people here, every day. Thousands of monsters. Red should stand out, somehow, in some way, but he doesn't—not among the gorgons with braided hair and mermaids being carted around in tanks. Red, out of everyone, is probably the most normal person here.

But he's still not quite human.

When he comes back, I split the scone in half, and he very obviously takes the larger piece. I lean on him slightly and cross my legs.

"I'm going to stop coming for a while," I say. He snaps over to look at me, and concern is so out of place on him that I have to laugh. "What?"

"What do you mean, what? You're leaving?"

I don't know what to tell him. No? I'm going to stick around here forever and wait for someone who may never come? I'm going to be bored stupid by spending hours in an *airport lobby* looking for jobs?

"I have an interview." I cross my legs and turn away. "And— you know. I don't want to—"

I stop myself before I can say "end up like you," but that's all I want to say. When I look at Red, I'm not looking at *Red* Red. I'm looking at *The Guy* Red. Which all makes sense in my head, somehow—something about him being a sad man, a shell, half a believer in something he was a skeptic about only a moment ago. But I'm seeing the wrong end of him, like reading a book upside down. I don't know him at all.

And there's no point in hanging around a permanent stranger.

"You don't want to?" he prompts. I shrug.

"What were you like before you came here?" I ask. I try to imagine him in a T-shirt, and suddenly feel a bit more comfortable.

The hair, at least, would make sense with an ugly shirt.

"A lot happier," he says, and then covers his mouth. "Oops." His eyes crinkle at the corners. "I don't think prophets should tell the truth, do you?"

"Happier?" I say, because he sure seems fine to me. Well, not fine—most people don't tell weird anti-prophet self-deprecating jokes—but fine enough. He eats scones, which is really the only necessary measure of fine-ness.

"More fulfilled," he says. "Suffused with energy? I don't know; what do you want me to tell you?"

"That you're quitting," I say. "And you're going to help me with my interview."

"Wear a suit."

"Not helpful," I say, but I'm smiling, and I do own a suit. Maybe I'll even wear it. "But back to my question. What would it take to make you leave?"

"Give me the person that I'm looking for," he says, and faces forward again.

I find it pretty hard to argue with that, so I just monsterwatch for another few minutes before getting up and dusting off my jeans. Stretching, I squint out across the lobby. The lights are just—so goddamn bright. Who designs these things.

When I turn to leave, Red jerks out of what looks like an open-eyed sleep.

"Goodbye," he says, and I look down at him.

"What?" I say.

"Goodbye," he repeats. "I—I never tell you goodbye."

Interesting. I walk closer to get a better angle on his expression, and it's not so bad. Maybe genuine. His eyes are a much darker grey than I thought they were.

"What are you doing?" he asks, and I lean back again.

"You looked weird there for a second. 'Bye."

And when I turn away, he almost seems confused. Which, to be fair, makes sense.

**

I spend a couple days at home, doing summer assignments and job-searching again. I look up a whole bunch of search terms—'red games' 'red video games' 'red video game development'—and find absolutely nothing, which was probably the point of the moniker to begin with. I figure that, without his real name, I can't find out anything, which kind of sucks, because I was planning on playing his video games. Or at least finding a demo.

In the meanwhile, I have a lot of time to think. A lot of time to lie on my bed and watch dust motes drift by. They're aimless and lazy; glowing in the light. Sometimes I can see constellations in them.

My interview went fine, by the way. I have another in three days. I'm alone in my bed, and Red's alone in the airport. Alone and surrounded by people, monsters, probably others. What's the point of him being there? What's the point of me being here? What's the point of me being anywhere, which sounds half-suicidal but isn't supposed to?

At least I'll have footage to edit soon. The people with the sitcom like me; I'll probably end up clipping out their coughs and bad takes. Mouse movement. Key pressing. Snippets of time drifting away.

**

The last time I come to the airport, I'm not sure how long it's been since Red said goodbye. It feels like a week or a month or some kind of unidentifiable not-quite-as-long-as-I-think-it-is stretch of time, and the tiles of the lobby floor click under my heels as I look for Red, who is not where he usually is, but definitely still here.

In the end, I run into him coming back from Cinnabon, and he looks very surprised and sort of pleased, but then he says "I only got one donut," and I tell him it's fine, we'll share, and then he just stares at me as I grab his lapels and drag him over to our usual spot.

"Someone's very excited today," he says, rearranging himself hurriedly.

"It's *me*," I say. He flattens part of his suit, looking very unruffled.

"I know it's you," he says. "I'm very aware; hence my comment directed *at you*—"

"I'm the *person*," I say. "Your fated person; your—whoever it is, it's *me.*"

Now he gapes at me. I guess I expected him to be more proactive about this.

"Also, I got a job," I say, and at least that shakes him far enough out of his whatever-it-is to wish me a mechanic congratulations.

Then several moments pass with me just sort of staring at him and him holding his donut, wearing a suit, looking surprised in his airport seat. Which is, by the way, not even close to the strangest situation we've been in.

"I think I would know," he says eventually, "if it was you."

"*I* know," I say. "It is me."

And then I sit down, and I take his donut out of his hands and eat it. Red just sits quietly and processes.

I don't actually know where I want to go from here—what I want to do. I want to get out of here, obviously, but I also want to figure things out. I want to learn Red's name, go for a run, look up more prophecy stuff, accept that I guess I'm mostly not a skeptic anymore; I want to *go*. I have a job, and a new camera, and I'm thinking of moving apartments, and there's so much to do and see and figure out, and Red is doing his best impression of a rock.

"Please get out of here with me," I say, and Red looks up at me. He narrows his eyes slightly, and I blink.

"Is that a date?" he asks.

"What."

"A *date,*" he says. "One of those things attractive people are supposed to ask me out on. We go play video games together, or we see a movie. A date."

"No," I say. "Yes. No. Only if you buy me another donut."

He looks at me, and I take a breath and fiddle with my hair.

"Which is it?" he says after a moment, and I reaffirm, "the donut."

So he gets up slowly, stretching in his stupid formal suit, and I dust off the seats before we walk away. People and monsters alike walk around us, and I take his hand gently to keep from losing him. Sometimes Red reflexively looks around, but he always glances back to me.

"You okay?" I ask, waiting for the line to shift. He nods and squeezes my hand.

"I'm okay."

The line moves forward, and I look back—the lobby's just as busy as ever. The peach-haired airport worker comes around to check on Red, and looks confusedly around himself when he finds no one.

blood orange tea.

Mel drinks coffee, tea, apple juice, orange juice, mango-raspberry smoothies, and water, but not fresh human blood. The context you are looking for here is that he is a vampire who works in a cafe.

Other important pieces of context: it is seven PM, he is locked into said cafe, and because he is stupid and morally adamant, he has not had any kind of blood in three days—which is really the limit for any solid-thinking vampire. Mel has read stories of vampires waiting longer, but those end in death as often as they do in undeath. Or life, or however it is Mel's breed of vampires are existing.

Another thing you might be interested in is the girl who works the same shift as Mel. Her name is *JENNY*, according to her little clip-on name tag, and she wipes tables with special kind of determined vigor.

Jenny's dark haired, and a combination of light- and dark-skinned in different places, and she brings little metal puzzles to work every day. When business is slow, sometimes Mel catches her solving them behind the counter; hoops and chains flying up and down, inside and across each other, linking together and apart. Like a kind of magic.

SOMETHING'S NOT RIGHT

Jenny's not the type of woman Mel expected would get him into this kind of situation, and he's not prepared to get himself out of it.

"Awfully dark out now," Jenny comments, in her pretty accent. Mel nods, and concentrates on breathing quietly and evenly. Or whatever passes for breathing his end of the vampire-biology setup; most vampire insides are complex and entirely decorative.

You know, he tries to be a good vampire. He spends the night in a tree outside the graveyard and gets blood bags from hospitals—hospitals he donates to anonymously online or leaves crumpled twenty-dollar bills in the storerooms of. He's never actually tried drinking blood from humans, and he keeps all his things in a little suitcase in his house-tree. He owns exactly one hat.

He is not the kind of vampire who deserves to starve to death in the middle of a cafe at nine fifteen at night.

"Sorry about all this," Jenny adds, and Mel remembers that she's probably at fault for most of it. He doesn't really feel anger. Or anything else, for that matter; his fingers are getting sort of numb at the ends. Usually he'd already be drinking by now.

"It's fine," Mel finds himself saying. "Sometimes you need to use the bathroom. And you need someone to watch the door for you."

yves.

(And you need all that to happen *exactly at closing time.*)

"Shame Belinda can't come back to open up," Jenny adds, and Mel looks at her.

He can't tell her he's a vampire. Technically, Mel shouldn't be telling Jenny *anything*—he's a vampire, she's a human, something something wanting to drink her blood and also maybe kiss her? He is afraid to think about the second part because it might lead to the first.

Either way, Mel is an Anti-Social Vampire. He has put that on literally every piece of social (ha) media he owns, and he intends to keep that as his label. Anti-Social. Very Safe. Very In Control Of His Vampiric Urges.

"I have—business," he says, anyway. "Urgently. Outside of this cafe.

"I'm sorry," Jenny says, and shifts sort of uncomfortably. "Um—do you want to... break a window?"

"No!" Mel thinks for a moment. "And we can't do that anyway; Belinda got one of those unbreakable-glass things and—it's fine, I don't—"

He doesn't have an excuse for needing to leave. Mel isn't generally adept in this department.

"It's fine," he finishes. Maybe he will be fine.

Around ten, Jenny starts yawning, and Mel pulls off his grey sweatshirt to give her something to use as a blanket. She insists that she's *not* tired and that she *doesn't* need to sleep, but Mel sits down behind the counter and refuses to speak to her until she's sitting beside him with the sweatshirt draped over her like a backwards cape.

"This is—violently soft," she says, leaning back against the drawers. Her head hits a handle. "Ow."

"Sorry," Mel says, and he sort of pulls her onto him, using his other hand to anxiously clutch his knees. This is almost certainly against something in the employee conduct handbook. It's *definitely* against something in every one of those Vampire Codes Mel has seen online.

Jenny doesn't seem bothered; she's out in seconds. Mel sits there, leaning his head back against the drawers, feeling Jenny's very human weight against his shoulder.

What Mel should be doing, right now, is going online to give generous donations to the hospital after stealing a not-insignificant amount of blood. Except he didn't exactly get around to that tonight, and now it looks like he isn't going to, and Jenny's skin is almost uncomfortably warm where it just barely touches him. Mel usually isn't good with heat, but Jenny's is strangely soothing.

System check: Mel is... lightheaded. Maybe. He's not sure if he really is or if he just thinks he is, or if it might be some kind of placebo effect, but he doesn't really have his full thinking capacities out right now. His fingers definitely feel numb. Other than that, it looks like most of him is doing an okay job of making it through the night.

Jenny wakes up eventually, and doesn't appear to remember where they are. Mel, actually, is growing (very slowly) less and less aware of his surroundings.

"Ow," Jenny mumbles. "My *neck.*"

She rubs at it, and Mel tries not to look. He feels very perverse.

"I'm sorry about your neck," he manages, and Jenny half-smiles.

"It's—fine. Did you get any sleep?"

"Yes," Mel lies. "A little."

Jenny's face is sort of swimming in front of him.

"You doing okay?"

Mel could eat a cow.

"I'm alright," he mumbles. Jenny leans in and puts two fingers under his chin, tilting his head up to face her. Mel does what he thinks is the vampire equivalent of sweating.

"You look awful," she murmurs. Mel *feels* a little awful. He's thinking a lot about blood, despite desperate attempts to ignore the subject. Jenny tilts his head side to side, performing what seems to be a thorough examination, and hums in concern. "I knew someone was going to get sick this week, but I didn't think it would be you."

Mel squints at her.

"I had a premonition," Jenny explains. Her eyes search his, and he nods. Sometimes people have those things. "I'm clairvoyant."

"Professionally?" Mel asks, because there's no more important question. Jenny's face changes, and she looks away.

"Used to be."

Mel doesn't know how to respond to this, and doesn't think he can, so he just offers his shoulder to her for the second time. She accepts, and leans back with a sigh.

It's one in the morning.

Mel pats Jenny's side absentmindedly. There are several hours left until the shop opens. The hospital is obviously *still* technically 'open' (at least to vampires who are sneaking in and stealing blood), but Mel has no way of getting there.

"I've been meaning to ask you—" Jenny turns her head slightly so as to make eye contact with Mel. Actually, it's not really eye contact; Mel's vision is going in and out of focus in patches.

Here it goes, he thinks. She's going to ask him if he's gay. This happens every time he gets even mildly close to someone. It does make sense, actually; he dresses like a cross between a priest and a raver, and only the cross is ironic. He's bi, but what does that matter—

"—are you a vampire?"

Oh.

Oh, whoops.

Mel isn't even present enough to register how much trouble he's in.

"I'm human," he murmurs, and Jenny puts a hand up to his forehead.

"Wow," she says. "No. No, you're not."

"I *am,*" Mel insists. His sight clears suddenly, and he blinks.

"Sure," she says. "I bet you don't drink blood either, huh?"

"No," Mel says, feeling empty.

Jenny frowns at him. He looks at her, holding her gaze as best he can. The conversation they're having seems better suited to a properly-fed Mel, one who can keep up with talking and secrets and whatnot.

"You look tired," Jenny says, and her voice is soft and concerned. She pulls Mel over so that he's leaning on her, and he breathes shallowly against her shoulder. Mel's sweatshirt isn't quite large enough to cover two, but she manages. "Maybe you are human, after all."

"Or maybe I haven't had any blood in the past three days," Mel whispers, waiting for his mind to catch up to his mouth. "Oh—"

"A-*ha*," Jenny says, pulling him closer. She rubs his arm slightly, and some feeling returns to him. He wishes he wasn't too focused on blood to smell her perfume. Suddenly, Jenny pulls back, and Mel is roughly shoved aside. "Wait—you haven't had any blood? In three *days?* Come on, you need to—"

And she pulls her sweater out of the way, revealing several inches of warm, soft skin. Mel puts his hand up to shield his eyes and immediately feels like an idiot. A morally secure idiot, though.

"Oh, my God," Jenny says, and she tugs at his hand gently. "Come *on.* How do you—how are you even alive without blood?"

"I'm not," Mel whispers. "Not technically."

yves.

"Not the time!" Jenny moves to sit in front of him. "Really—you don't look okay. If you don't get blood, you'll—"

"Die. Yes." Mel leans back and closes his eyes. "I'll be fine."

"No you won't—Mel, I cannot believe I am arguing with you over *dying.*"

"Your accent makes this a lot funnier," Mel says, very quietly, and it's really a dick move, but he's hours from death so it's kind of acceptable.

A pause follows that's so long he worries Jenny's left. He opens his eyes to find her giving him a truly unreadable expression.

"You're an idiot," she says, and, coincidentally, her accent makes that a lot funnier, too.

"Just—let's try and wait this out," Mel says. "Maybe I can make it through the night."

Jenny stands and starts rooting around through different drawers behind the counter. Mel watches for a moment before asking what on earth she's doing.

"In case you *don't* make it—" She grabs a pair of scissors from one of the drawers, and Mel scrambles up from the floor to pin her against the counter and grab the scissors out of her hands. It's surprisingly easy; for all her strength and his blood loss (if that's even what it's called for vampires) he's still not human. It's like fighting with a mouse.

"Don't," he says, and he gets a little lightheaded as he says it. His hands shake where he's holding Jenny back. "Ah."

"Don't exert yourself," Jenny mutters, and shoves him off her. He stumbles back, sort of sliding down the cupboards on the opposite wall. He sends Jenny a wary glance, and she looks at the scissors oddly. Her hands shake.

"Oh my God," Mel says, half-smiling. He laughs quietly. "You're scared."

"I'm not," Jenny says, in a tone absolutely unfit for the statement. 'I—I'll do it if I have to."

"You won't have to." Mel makes a small noise and closes his eyes, trying to get a more comfortable position up against the cupboards. "I'll be fine."

There's a quick clanking sound as Jenny drops the scissors on the counter, and Mel can't tell what she's doing for a moment. Then he hears her drop down beside him, and suddenly she's pulling his head into her lap. It's slightly uncomfortable, and then much more comfortable.

"If I said my last wish was for you to end the peppermint

flavor," he whispers, "would you do it?"

"Absolutely not," she says, and laughs quietly. "I don't think I even have that power."

There's a ticking clock somewhere above their heads, and Mel tries to guess the time. It's possible he'll be able to hold out until daylight, and then it'll be nothing to just walk over and steal the blood in the morning—provided he wears his sunscreen, and probably also that someone holds him up—but the sky outside is still cerulean blue, and the dawn can't possibly come fast enough. Belinda comes in to open the shop at 5:00; Mel is going to die here.

He really should be much less calm about that.

"Mel," Jenny whispers, and Mel sort of comes to. He doesn't think he's been sleeping, precisely, but he certainly hasn't been tuned into the world for the past few... however long it's been.

"Yes?"

"Have you ever bitten someone before?"

"No."

"Oh."

Mel closes his eyes again, and Jenny giggles quietly.

"What?"

"Oh, nothing." Mel waits, and Jenny does this quiet little laugh before continuing. "But I think that explains it."

"What, that I don't want to injure someone, *drink* their *blood*—"

"It's not that much blood." Jenny pauses, and Mel can hear her quiet breath in the shop. The air is very cold, though of course that means nothing to him. "Is it?"

"I don't know." Mel uses his ornamental respiratory system to sigh dramatically, because it feels like a very nice way to punctuate his statements. "Like I said—I've never bitten anyone."

"Can you do it wrong?" Mel doesn't answer, and Jenny's fingers tighten on his shoulders. "Mel?" She shakes him slightly. *"Mel—"*

"I don't know!" He turns his head slightly. "I don't know. I think it's instinctual."

He *thinks* it's instinctual, because every passing moment he has a greater urge to do it. Jenny is hovering above him, and she smells so *human,* and she's breathing so gently. She *wants* him to bite her. She's as close as Mel can get to a sitting duck.

"You should try it."

"I couldn't," he says, and an angry knot of fear joins the hunger already coiling around his veins.

"Why *not,*" Jenny asks, and she shakes him rather urgently, and he doesn't know how to answer her. Isn't it so cliché of him to fear he'll take too much?

"I don't have any idea what I'm doing, and I'm *very* hungry, and you're just going to die." Mel takes a strong breath; he needs something to occupy himself that isn't passing out. "I don't want you to die," he manages.

(Romance.)

"I didn't foresee myself dying. I'll be fine." Jenny tucks a curl of her hair behind her ear. She looks very calm, actually, except around the eyes.

"You didn't foresee me being sent to the brink of death, either." Mel blinks a couple times. "Did you foresee us getting stuck in here together?"

"I had a premonition that the dove and the owl would roost together until dawn." Jenny pets Mel's blonde hair softly. "Does that mean my subconscious sees me as an owl?"

"I'm more worried about my being a dove. You're too trusting."

"You don't trust yourself enough. How are you?"

It takes Mel a moment to realize she's asking physically, and also to figure out how to respond. The space behind his eyes is buzzing, and his arms feel limp, and he's not sure whether his fangs are out or not.

"Not well," he says, because in addition to all of this, it also feels like his veins are singing, and not in a positive way.

Jenny pulls him closer, leaning his head on her chest. Her heart is beating. Mel looks past her to the full-length windows of the cafe, watching the midnight city go by; it must be almost two by now, but it still feels like it's midnight, and the crows on the sidewalk are unnatural and strange. Mel leans his face further into Jenny's shoulder, and she puts her hand on the back of his head.

"I had a shop," she says. "Witching sort of thing. Tarot cards, lucky charms, all that and whatnot."

She takes a deep breath, and Mel looks up at her.

"What happened?" he asks.

Jenny has the darkest lashes of anyone Mel's ever seen. They brush against her cheeks and flit lightly up and down as she thinks.

"I lost it," she says, eventually. Too sharply. "I had these— mandatory reportings, and I—I just kept acting out. Tosser named Jared gave my job to someone else."

She grits her teeth, which momentarily seem sharper than Mel's.

yves.

"Probably very happy with his new oracle," she mutters. Mel does whatever can plausibly be called both hugging and not hugging.

If he squints, he thinks he can see a brightening on the horizon.

Jenny tilts her head back against the cabinets, and Mel can see the long expanse of her neck as a saturated silhouette against her hair. Her skin is dark there, climbing up to the pale spots around her chin and mouth. Mel watches that slender neck take in breath; examines the planes and ridges of her throat. There are scars and tick-marks against her skin, so small they can barely be noticed, but altogether there.

"I'll do it," he says, and it's only then that he realizes she's been crying.

"What?" Jenny manages, and her voice is scratchy and raw. Mel looks away briefly; he feels more than sees her wipe at her eyes.

"Your blood," he says. "If—you really—"

"Yes," Jenny says, immediately, and moves away to take a cross-legged seat before him. Mel swoons almost instantly, finding himself lightheaded and more tired than he's ever been in his life/undeath, and Jenny grabs at his arms to steady him.

"Oops," he says, and sort of smiles up at her, but both of their expressions are strained.

"Be careful," Jenny says, and for a second there's a flash of worry in her eyes. Mel can feel her shallow breathing in his skin.

He moves forward, tipping her head slightly to the left, and her breath resounds against his light skin. He closes his eyes briefly, concentrating; being so long without blood has robbed him of whatever kind of sense he might have been able to use. Doing this so late was *stupid,* if he'd agreed earlier it might have been safer—better—

"Mel?" she whispers, and her voice is so scared and so quiet. Mel hesitates, but her perfume is intoxicating. Something sweeter than candy; pink and soft. He leans in and bites her.

He didn't expect live blood to taste better or worse than the donated stuff he keeps getting, or really the same either, but it's *warm,* and that alone can make all the difference; her blood is whisper-soft and warm-threaded, bruise-red in an unforgivingly fleeting way, and he has to keep drinking and drinking, and Jenny is clinging to him, nails digging into his skin, and if he's going to have scars forever then he's going to have scars forever because he deserves it—this is worth it—

"Stop," Jenny whispers, and Mel pulls back. He's horrified, for a moment, at Jenny's glazed eyes, then proud of his own self-control, then violently repulsed by what he is. What he's become. Jenny blinks several times, and they lock eyes, and then Mel and Jenny are holding each other, and the shop is silent, and they are both in pieces.

Jenny is crying. Mel, being a vampire, cannot cry, but what he is doing isn't any different.

"You've gotten blood all over my shirt," Jenny murmurs, pulling back, and Mel realizes that he *has,* oh God, and she just sort of bats at it uselessly. Mel hands her his sweatshirt, and she stands and walks into the bathroom to change, and Mel is left sitting wide-eyed on the shop floor. There are coffee beans on the floor around him, despite all of their sweeping, and the air suddenly smells sharp with it. The sound of running water comes from the restroom. Mel wishes he could breathe properly.

He drank her blood.

Jenny returns looking inappropriately domestic in Mel's soft grey sweatshirt. He stares up at her in horror, and she looks down at him with a startling neutrality. The wound on her neck has been covered with a nondescript, pastel-peach Band-Aid; it looks just like any other place on her skin where her body fades into lightness.

"I'm sorry," Mel manages, and Jenny shakes her head. Mel looks away when she sits down beside him, and his head is burning with the fact of what he's just done. He's filled with a kind of clarity hunger stole from him, and he half-wishes he wasn't.

"It's fine," Jenny says, and it is *not* fine, but if she wants to pretend then Mel will let her. "Being bitten was—on my bucket list, actually. So this is good."

'So this is good.'

This is—not good, Mel wants to say. *This is broken, this is awful. This is not what I wanted to be for you and what I always knew I would become in the end. This is a mistake, and I should never have come here.*

The worst part is that he knows she's going to try to befriend him now, and he won't have the strength to resist her. Not like before.

Mel must look upset, or angry, or cocooned in a shell of negative emotions (all of which he feels), because Jenny shrugs and stands, stretching.

"I would've broken the window," she says, and Mel looks up at her as she leans one stocking-clad leg against the counter. She bends to retie her shoe, nonchalant. "If you wanted me to."

yves.

"I know," Mel says.

But it's too late now, anyway. Even if it had been possible to begin with.

Jenny looks out the window, and Mel glances out to join her. The crow he saw earlier has been joined by several friends, and they peck together at different invisible spots on the ground. Pigeonlike.

"Seven of them," Jenny says, and when Mel doesn't immediately understand, she points to the crows. "Like the Seven of Wands."

Mel doesn't read tarot, but he can see, and—

"Those are crows, not wands," he says, wiping the blood from his mouth.

Jenny turns and gives him a smile at once derisive and endeared. It's secretive enough that he doesn't question her any further.

By the time Belinda arrives, Mel can't wait to leave, and Jenny is left to give the hour-long explanation. Mel feels bad over it, though at the moment it's not anything he or she can worry about.

He takes a week off sick and buys an apartment. His search history fills up with advice forums for vampires, small cat photos, and tarot card listings on foreign sites. He considers buying the cards, too, before realizing that he's being an idiot about things.

Though Jenny would undoubtedly like tarot cards better than flowers.

When Mel comes back to work, it's as a customer first; he walks in at a time when he knows Jenny will be on shift. And she's there, in her apron, writing someone's name on their cup and nodding. Mel realizes he looks like a creep, lingering in the doorway, and gets in line.

When Mel hits the front of the line, Jenny stops. Her hand hovers over the register; Mel's gaze flies immediately to her neck. There's no bandage; she must heal fast. He pauses, and clears his throat awkwardly.

"Um," he says, and she smiles. He tries to think of what to say and can't, which means he's sort of out of it when she speaks.

"Café au lait with extra sugar and whipped cream." Jenny looks at him for confirmation, pen poised over the cup, and Mel actually takes a step back.

"You—know," he says, because he's ordered from Jenny exactly once (before he started working) and she's not supposed to notice him. Jenny shrugs, smiling. She's so unbelievably pretty.

It takes Mel a minute to realize that she's waiting for

confirmation, so he nods and stumbles through some kind of yes-related statement with a lot of "ums" strung into it, and she scribbles his name onto the cup. Then she pauses, and adds something.

Mel watches as Jenny turns the cup around to show how she's written his name: in her signature thick, blocky handwriting, with the legs of the *M* pointing in to make a small, round heart.

acknowledgements.

To my friends Kay, Lo, Riley, Derron, and Celia for advice, sensitivity readings, and edits; along with Avery, Allen, Renard, Bentley, Nat, Danny, Rysz, Jun, and Anna, for the obvious moral support:

To older influences, who told me I could write and who are now only ghosts; T., J., J., S., and R.; Hope, Sydney, Sabrina, Shiraa, Liam and Anna, (who technically also belong here, though they're much more corporeal):

To people I must still address with polite honorifics and who did many different things, particularly Rabbi Greenberg (thank you for buying a story), Dr. Janda (thank you for reading a story, and before that, encouraging Lons and Flos), Ms. McElhatton (thank you for also putting up with frankendad), Mr. Marmer (thank you for the writing space), Ms. Warren (thank you for the thoughts), Mr. Ribay (this book wouldn't exist *at all* without you and you have completely changed the way I write for the better... stakes! conflict!), Ms. Woodham (for letting me spoil one of my stories, and reading it anyway), and Moshe (who has ruined my exceptionally funny joke about honorifics, but is excused because of how happy he makes me [and everyone else] whenever he is around):

To the 'mates, absolutely including those who are now gone, for helping me up:

(Something religious enough to be identifiably Jewish, but not so concrete that people assume I know anything about God for certain):

To my fellow LGBT folks, monstrous or otherwise:

Thank you.

—yves.

about the author.

yves. is bisexual, attractive, non-human, confused, and brown-haired, in that order. after that, yves. is a prolific writer and an avid cat-owner, again in that order, and after that, yves. is pronounced 'yves dot' and always written lowercase. anything more can be learned through following yves on yvesdot.tumblr.com, medium.com/@yvesdot, or twitter.com/yvesdot, as well as taking a look at bit.ly/snrgoodreads. alternatively, mail is accepted at allhallowsyves@gmail.com.

Made in the USA
San Bernardino, CA
16 May 2018